HIEROGLYPHS OF HORROR

www.**stevecolebooks**.co.uk

Also by Steve Cole:

ASTROSAURS

Riddle of the Raptors
The Hatching Horror
The Seas of Doom
The Mind-Swap Menace
The Skies of Fear
The Space Ghosts
Day of the Dino-Droids
The Terror-Bird Trap
The Planet of Peril
The Star Pirates
The Claws of Christmas
The Sun-Snatchers
Revenge of the Fang
The Carnivore Curse
The Dreams of Dread
The Robot Raiders
The Twist of Time
The Sabre-Tooth Secret
The Forest of Evil
Earth Attack!
The T-Rex Invasion
The Castle of Frankensaur

ASTROSAURS ACADEMY

Destination: Danger!
Contest Carnage!
Terror Underground!
Jungle Horror!
Deadly Drama!
Christmas Crisis!
Volcano Invaders!
Space Kidnap!

COWS IN ACTION

The Ter-Moo-nators
The Moo-my's Curse
The Roman Moo-stery
The Wild West Moo-nster
World War Moo
The Battle for Christmoos
The Pirate Moo-tiny
The Moogic of Merlin
The Victorian Moo-ders
The Moo-lympic Games
First Cows on the Mooon
The Viking Emoo-gency

The Udderly Moo-vellous
C.I.A. Joke Book

Astrosaurs vs Cows in Action:
The Dinosaur Moo-tants

SLIME SQUAD

The Fearsome Fists
The Toxic Teeth
The Cyber-Poos
The Supernatural Squid
The Killer Socks
The Last-Chance Chicken
The Alligator Army
The Conquering Conks

Secret Agent Mummy
The Cleopatra Case

For older readers:

Z. Rex
Z. Raptor
Z. Apocalypse

Young Bond: Shoot to Kill

HIEROGLYPHS OF HORROR

STEVE COLE

Illustrated by Donough O'Malley

RED FOX

For Peter Kittel

SECRET AGENT MUMMY: THE HIEROGLYPHS OF HORROR
A RED FOX BOOK 978 1 849 41871 3

First published in Great Britain by Red Fox,
an imprint of Random House Children's Publishers UK
A Penguin Random House Company

Penguin
Random House
UK

This edition published 2016

1 3 5 7 9 10 8 6 4 2

Text copyright © Steve Cole, 2016
Logo artwork copyright © Andy Parker, 2014
Cover artwork copyright © Dave Shelton, 2016
Interior illustrations copyright © Donough O'Malley, 2016
Ancient Egypt Advisor – Louise Ellis-Barrett

Penguin Random House is committed to a sustainable future for our business, our readers
and our planet. This book is made from Forest Stewardship Council® certified paper.

MIX
Paper from
responsible sources
FSC
www.fsc.org
FSC® C018179

Set in Bembo MT Schoolbook

Red Fox Books are published by Random House Children's Publishers UK,
61–63 Uxbridge Road, London W5 5SA

www.**stevecolebooks**.co.uk
www.**randomhousechildrens**.co.uk
www.**totallyrandombooks**.co.uk
www.**randomhouse**.co.uk

Addresses for companies within The Random House Group Limited can be found at:
www.randomhouse.co.uk/offices.htm

THE RANDOM HOUSE GROUP Limited Reg. No. 954009

A CIP catalogue record for this book is available from the British Library.

Printed and bound in Great Britain by CPI Group (UK) Ltd, Croydon, CR0 4YY

Did you know that Ancient Egypt was once home to THINGS from another UNIVERSE?

These MYSTERIOUS visitors from the realm of KaBa inspired the old Egyptians, who treated them like gods. But EVIL, BAD, FREAKY CREATURES also came to stay – so BIONIC SECRET AGENTS from KaBa were sent to catch them.

Thousands of years later, ONE of those secret agents is STILL on the case. Because SPOOKY MONSTERS are still on the loose ...

In these pages you will meet:

SAM

Brave, bold – but not very bright, Sam is the only Secret Agent Mummy still fighting crime all over our world. His super-tough bandages protect him from enemy attacks and the passing years – he is thousands of years old! He lives in a portable Pyra-Base, hidden from human eyes. With magic, might, cool in-built weapons and a LOT of good luck, he blunders through adventures with the help of his friends . . .

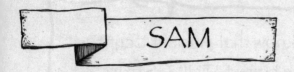

MEW

This snooty cat goddess is the brains of Sam's outfit. She stayed on Earth because she loves the taste of fish! Annoying and vain, she will only help out on anti-bad-guy operations in exchange for worship and cod.

MUMBUM

This semi-robotic dog was once Sam's loyal hunting hound, until he met with a terrible accident. Only his bottom survived. Now wrapped in bandages, Mumbum can be strapped into different metal bodies for different situations – the ultimate utility pooch.

NIALL RIVERS

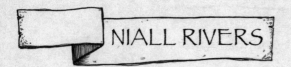

One fateful day, Niall found a magical relic from KaBa, touched it — and absorbed its powers! As a result, Niall is the only human able to see Sam's secret world. He has become Sam's special sidekick, helping him on his mad mummy adventures. Quick-thinking, courageous and good with gadgets — both those from Earth and those from KaBa — Niall shares Sam's mission to protect the world from incredible dangers.

NOW, LET THE ADVENTURE BEGIN . . .

Chapter One

A Rubbish Robbery

"RIGHT!" Niall Rivers couldn't take any more. "That *does* it!"

His annoying little sister, Ellie – also known as the Snitch – had taken the last of the good cereal, leaving only Mum's gross muesli for breakfast . . . Then she drank the last of the orange juice . . . Now, she was sticking her

tongue out at him.

"Hungry for more, huh?" Niall lifted a spoonful of his oaty mush and flicked it at her face. *SPLAT!* "There!"

"Mum!" The Snitch shrieked, her blonde bunches trembling. "Look what Niall did!"

Mum sighed from behind the local newspaper. "Be nice to your sister, Niall."

"Maybe one day." Niall grinned at the Snitch. "Anything good in the paper, Mum?

Like evil aliens visiting earth and abducting little sisters?"

"Don't be ridiculous," Mum said.

It could happen, Niall thought to himself.

In fact, it *had* happened – just a few weeks ago!

He smiled. Incredible, impossible adventures were never far away when you lived next door to someone as incredible and impossible as Sam . . .

Of course, Sam wasn't just any old neighbour. The three letters of his nickname – S, A, M – stood for Secret Agent Mummy; almost

 3

three thousand years old and covered from head to toe in bandages, this ancient detective from a far-off realm had fought crime in Ancient Egypt – and had continued to fight it (or continued *trying* to fight it) ever since.

Since Sam was a *secret* agent, no one was meant to know any of this. But just a few months ago, Niall had got caught up in one of Sam's investigations. He'd stumbled across a magical Egyptian relic and accidentally absorbed its powers! Now he could see things that other people

4

couldn't — like Sam's home, the Pyra-Base: a massive magical sandstone pyramid that was parked in next-door's garden. And his natural skill with gadgets had been amplified to mega-levels, so that he could even understand the bonkers technology from Sam's world . . .

"Every story in this rag sounds ridiculous!" Mum lowered her news-paper, and caught the Snitch wiping cereal off her face. She frowned. "Ellie, what have you done?"

5

"I told you," the Snitch whined, "it was Niall!"

"It's not my fault if you can't eat your breakfast without getting half of it all over your face!" Niall shot back with a grin.

"Honestly, you two!" Mum threw down the paper. "Come on, Ellie, you've got dance class this morning – it's time we were getting dressed."

As the Snitch followed Mum out of the kitchen, she glared at Niall. "Bum-head," she mouthed at him.

Niall shrugged. "I know you are!"

He glanced down at the newspaper and a

6

headline caught his eye: SOUVENIR SNATCHERS! Burglars had broken into an old man's house, but all they had taken was a box of keepsakes from his recent Nile cruise.

"Probably the most rubbish robbery of all time," Niall murmured, reading on. The box – private property of one Mr Hoyle – apparently contained postcards, a stuffed toy camel, a model pyramid . . . and a small round stone, discovered near the Great Pyramid of Giza.

Niall studied the picture in the paper more closely. It was a photo of the missing stone – round and smooth like an eyeball and marked

with an Egyptian symbol Niall recognized as the forelegs of an ox – the hieroglyph meaning "power".

"That's no ordinary stone," Niall breathed. It looked like something from Sam's world, the realm of KaBa. And if it was powerful, it could be dangerous . . .

I'd better show this report to Sam, he thought.

Once Mum and the Snitch had left, Niall wrote a note to say he was going round to a friend's house, tucked the newspaper under his arm and went into the back garden. Over the fence, he could see Sam's Pyra-Base towering

over the tangled weeds in the garden of the empty house next door.

Funny, he thought, *it seems to be shimmering slightly*. It couldn't be a heat haze; it wasn't warm enough.

He climbed over the fence and jumped down the other side. Making his way towards the pyramid, he heard a sinister humming sound . . .

The Pyra-Base's triangular entrance was standing wide open. Inside, Niall could see a huge tangle of wires spilling from a hole in the wall like a waterfall of multicoloured spaghetti.

9

"I came here to talk about one weird Egyptian burglary," Niall muttered. "Now it looks like I've found another . . ."

Then he gasped. Because there on the ground, poking out from the mess of cables, were two large bandaged feet, twitching on the ends of similarly bandaged legs.

"Sam! Are you all right?" Niall charged

forward to try and help his friend. "What's happened here?"

But as he neared the Pyra-Base doorway – *Za-BOOOOM!* It was as if he'd run into an invisible bouncy castle.

An invisible *electrified* bouncy castle.

"ARRRGH!" In a glittering spray of sparks, Niall and his newspaper were thrown backwards through the air . . .

Chapter Two

Invisible Walls

Niall landed heavily in an overgrown flowerbed.

"Whoa!" Scrambling to his feet, he went back to the pyramid, more cautiously this time, his arms held out in front of him. "Sam, I'm trying to get to you, but— OW!" *Za-boom!* Niall's fingertips tingled and sparked and he pulled his hands back. Thinking quickly, he

returned to the flowerbed, picked up a clod of earth and flung it at the pyramid. It almost reached the doorway, but then ricocheted back at him in a blaze of light.

"It's some sort of energy barrier, sealing off the Pyra-Base!" Niall stared through the open doorway at the bandaged figure that was all but buried by the wires. "Hang in there, Sam, I'm coming to help you. I'll find another way in. I just hope this force-field doesn't go all the way round . . ."

Anxiously, Niall gathered stones and more mud from the flowerbed and set off round the

pyramid, throwing the mucky missiles now and then to see how far the invisible barrier stretched.

Ba-BOOOM! Ya-BOOOOOOM!

At last, about halfway round, a stone made contact with the Pyra-Base.

Or, to be exact, the stone made contact with one of the Pyra-Base's triangular windows.

SMASH! The glass shattered noisily.

"Finally!" Niall rushed forward, ready to climb inside.

But then: "MEEEEOOOOOWWWWW!"

With a screech, a white-and-gold blur burst out of the window, landed on Niall's face and

14

knocked him to the ground again!

"What the . . . ?" Spitting fur in disgust, Niall sat up – to find a thin white cat beside him. She was covered in gold bandages, with a tiara perched on her head.

"Mew, it's you!" Niall groaned. Like Sam, this cat had come to Ancient Egypt from KaBa thousands of years ago – and she had done nothing but eat fish and demand to be worshipped ever since. "Why did you pounce on me like that?"

"You threw a stone through the bathroom window while I was using the toilet, boy! I

thought you were an evil attacker!" The moggy bristled. "Anyway, that's *Great* Mew, to you. Have you forgotten that I'm descended from Bastet the cat-goddess?"

"Never mind all that," Niall panted. "Sorry to scare you, but I was just trying to get inside to help Sam. He's lying on the floor and the door's open and there's an invisible wall and—"

"*HOLD IT!*" Suddenly a hail of feathered darts shot over Niall's head and blasted into the pyramid wall and window, breaking the

last of the glass. Mew squealed and Niall threw himself to the ground. The darts stuck out of the sandstone like curious quills, as a familiar booming voice continued: "Whoever broke my window will taste my razor-sharp ostrich feathers!"

"Wait!" Niall turned to see a tall fierce-looking figure wearing a rain- coat, trousers and lots and lots of bandages; he looked ready for action. "Sam?"

"Niall Rivers?" The Secret Agent Mummy looked confused. "My young friend, it is good to ocean you."

"Good to *see* you back on your feet too." Niall got up shakily. "Although those flying feathers came a little too close for comfort."

"Forgive my hasty reaction." Sam bowed. "I heard Great Mew cry out. When I saw the broken window, I thought the Pyra-Base had come under fire before we could finish our protective energy shield."

"*Your* energy shield?" Niall groaned. "When I saw you lying under all those wires, I

18

thought you'd been attacked!"

"The shield is not yet working properly," Sam explained. "I was on the floor trying to fix it."

"It is vital that our shield surrounds the whole base as quickly as possible," Mew twittered. "I must be kept safe from danger!"

Sam nodded. "Strange plots loom over us, my friend. Come – I shall explain all!"

Chapter Three

Robbed of Power

"Danger?" Niall looked suspiciously at Mew. "Do you mean *real* danger, or are you just running out of fish?"

"Don't be so cheeky, you weak-minded window breaker!" Mew tutted crossly. "Apologize at once – by giving me one cod."

"No," said Niall flatly.

"Very well, pay for that window, then!"

Mew smiled. "Price: one cod!"

"The window was broken because the barrier is not yet strong enough to contain the whole of the Pyra-Base," Sam reminded Mew. "Niall is talented with gadgets. Perhaps he can make the shield stronger?"

Niall realized that the humming sound had stopped. "I'll have a look," he agreed. "But the Pyra-Base has been broken into before; if you've got a shield, why haven't you been using it?"

"The shield is powered by a Crystal of Ra," Sam revealed.

Niall had heard the name Ra in school

lessons. "Named after the Egyptian sun-god?"

"That's what you human fools thought he was." Mew gave a lofty shrug. "Really, Ra was just a very good electrician!"

"Crystals of Ra project energy through space – the Pyra-Base's system uses this energy to make a strong shield." Sam led the way back to the entrance. "Back in the seventeenth century, our Crystal of Ra mysteriously went missing. I only recently found a spare crystal in my Ancient Egyptian football boots."

"Didn't know you played football," said Niall.

"I used to play against my camels. But they are most competitive." Sam shivered. "I had to stop playing – every time they scored goals they did a victory dance right on top of me."

"Lucky you come ready-bandaged," said Niall.

"Yes, indeed!" Sam moved a mass of wires and lifted a sandstone brick in the floor to reveal a glowing red cavity. "Now, behold . . . my Crystal of Ra."

Niall stared at the glowing sphere inside, saw the symbols on its surface and felt a shiver run through him.

23

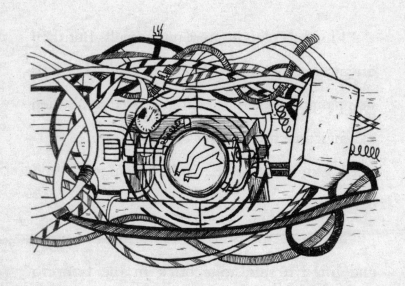

The forelegs of an ox: the Egyptian symbol for power!

"It's just like Mr Hoyle's stone in the paper!" He rushed back to the flowerbed, grabbed his crumpled newspaper, turned to the picture of

the old man's holiday souvenir and pushed it under Sam's bandaged nose. "I came over here to show you this: a Crystal of Ra that's been stolen."

Sam took the paper. "I did not steal it!"

"But someone else did." Mew peered at the picture. "I am aware of this report. I suspect this one came from a Pyra-Base that once stood in Giza."

"And an old *geezer* found it lying around." Niall turned to Mew. "So, who do you think stole it off poor old Mr Hoyle?"

"I do not know." The cat shook her head,

25

nearly losing her tiara. "But it is not the only Crystal of Ra to go missing. I shall explain more in the operations room – once you have fixed that shield!"

As she slunk away, Niall sighed and tried to make sense of the wire spaghetti. "So, this Crystal of Ra projects power through the air, right?"

"It is made of a special substance that draws energy from the sun," Sam revealed. "Take care never to spill water on one – or it will explode, *KA-BOOM!*"

"Thanks for the tip." Niall checked out the

cables, meters and gadgets plugged into the crystal. "These must control the energy supply. Aha! There's a loose connection." He quickly swapped some wires round. "There. Switch it on now."

Sam pressed a red button on the wall and the humming sound started up again, stronger and louder. "Success!" he cried, as a soft yellow glow appeared between them and the world outside. "Well done, my young friend! The Crystal of Ra is projecting its power! Now no one nasty can get inside."

"Apart from Mew, who's *already* inside."

Niall smirked. "Let's see what she has to say."

He followed Sam to the operations room, which was furnished with a strange mishmash of the ancient and the modern. The large space was lit by candles and torches, and filled with pyramid-shaped computers; triangular TV screens were fixed to the walls. There was a living area, a small stone kitchen with a sarcophagus for a fridge, and enough urns, gold and statues to fill a pharaoh's tomb. Niall loved the crazy mix of spooky tomb and future tech!

"So, boy . . ." Mew had settled herself on a sphinx-shaped sofa with a large haddock and

a triangular remote control. "You noticed that a Crystal of Ra had been stolen from close by. But have you noticed the other alarming robberies in the news recently?"

"No," Niall admitted.

"Well, we do have an advantage." Mew preened. "Our spy computers analyse human media and record any story that may involve technology from KaBa." She hit a button on the remote. "Here is a news report from last week in Northern Ireland . . ." A large screen

29

on the wall flickered and an image of a junk shop appeared, its front door hanging from twisted hinges.

". . . the shop was broken into, but all that was stolen was an old cracked stone with Egyptian markings . . ." the newsreader declared.

Niall raised his eyebrows as a picture of that "old cracked stone" flashed up on the screen. "A Crystal of Ra," he realized.

As the news changed, to a piece about animals that had gone missing from Belfast Zoo, Mew switched to another channel. "A larger crystal in better condition was recently stolen from a museum in London. Look!"

Niall saw the front page of a newspaper. PRICELESS RELIC SNATCHED! screamed the headline.

"What would anyone want with all these Crystal of Ra power projectors?" Niall pondered. "Can humans use them?"

"No," said Mew. "They only work with technology from KaBa."

31

"Look here, my friend. CROCODILES PETRIFIED MY POOCH!" read Sam, pointing to a smaller story in the London paper. "*An old woman walking her dog spotted dozens of crocodiles slithering into the sewers. The dog ran away and has not returned . . .*"

"That loopy lady and her mutt need not concern us!" Mew bit the head off her haddock. "Far more disturbing is the story you failed to spot in your local paper."

Sam held up Niall's copy. "Behold, my friend."

"An advert for Fat Barry's Pizza Shack?"

Niall asked in surprise.

"Forgive me! Wrong page." He smiled. "Although praised be their stuffed crusts and 'buy ten, get one half-price' offers!"

Sam turned the paper round, and Niall saw another story: "CAT CALAMITY! MYSTERY OF MISSING MOGGIES," he read aloud. "*Police are investigating the disappearance of forty cats from a cattery. The cage doors were clawed off from the inside . . .*"

"The cattery is just round the corner from Mr Hoyle's house." Mew shivered. "The cats vanished shortly before the old man was robbed

of his Crystal of Ra. Not one of them has been seen since."

"So *that's* why you've made Sam sort out the Pyra-Base's energy shield," said Niall. "You're worried *you* might get taken along with the Crystal of Ra!"

"And why shouldn't I worry?!" Mew snapped. "I am worth a thousand of those dreary old pussies!"

"And the Pyra-Base is full of wonderful things from KaBa," said Sam. "If this mysterious robber should find us . . ."

"He'll find the crystal he's come to steal is

powering the energy barrier that's keeping him out!" Niall smiled. "So what are you going to do? Sit tight behind your shield and hope he gets bored of his collecting hobby?"

"No!" Sam puffed out his bandaged chest and put on a pair of dark glasses. "I am going to outvestigate the crime scenes myself!"

"You mean, *in*vestigate?"

"No, my friend! Since I am going outside, I must be *out*vestigating! I am sure to find clues your human police have missed." Sam strode towards the door – but with his shades on he failed to notice the pyramid-shaped coffee table

in his path and tripped over it, crashing into some canopic jars. "Whoops! I think I just knocked over my lungs . . ."

Niall quickly helped him up. "Tell you what: why don't I come with you?"

"A splendid idea." Sam got to his feet. "Let us go at once."

Mew stretched out on the sofa and scoffed the rest of her haddock. "Mr Hoyle's house and the cattery are five miles from here. Call in at the fishmonger's on the way back and bring me a nice tasty cod, would you? MEOWW!"

But Niall wasn't listening. Sam had pulled

36

down the bandages that covered his ribcage to reveal a red stone — his ruby of transportation. "Next stop, the catless cattery!"

Light swirled out of the ruby's depths, and Niall felt it engulf them both . . .

The outvestigation had begun!

Chapter Four

A Mexican Outvestigator Calls

Niall had travelled by magic ruby before; it felt as if he was upside-down on a rollercoaster, while whizzing through a firework display. He landed beside Sam with a bump and the ruby's red light faded.

"We are arrived," said Sam.

They were standing outside a light, airy

building beside a sign that read, THE PUSS PALACE – YOUR CAT'S HOME FROM HOME. The gateway at the side of the house had been boarded up. The wooden gate itself was lying on its side, propped up against the wall; Niall saw that the lower section had been broken clean away, and the remaining wood was scored with deep scratches.

"Those cats must have been desperate to get out . . ." He looked at Sam – and did a double-take. Somehow, during the journey from the Pyra-Base, his friend had managed to change his outfit. He was now wearing a colourful wide-brimmed sombrero and a poncho. "Er,

Sam? Why are you dressed like that?"

"Is it not clear, my friend?" The mummy lowered his voice. "I am going under sheets."

"Under*cover*." Niall shook his head wearily. "But now you stand out a mile."

"Of course," Sam replied. "I am putting observers off the smell. When I climb into this back garden and search for empty cat-houses, they will say, 'No burglar would dress so crazy!

He must be a simple tourist from Japan who is lost.'"

"Sombreros come from Mexico!"

"A tourist from Japan who is *very* lost."

With that, Sam scrambled over the boarded-up gateway and disappeared from sight. Niall quickly followed him down the narrow path that ran alongside the building, and into the large, rather muddy garden area at the back.

It wasn't hard to see where the cats had been kept at night: rows of cages were torn apart and wire netting hung in shreds.

"Wow," said Niall. "If someone only wanted

 41

to take the cats, why cause so much damage?"

"Look here!" Sam pointed to strange prints in the mud near the cages.

Niall studied them. "They look like they were made by . . . I don't know – a dinosaur or something!"

"I have seen such marks before," Sam murmured. "In Egypt, long ago. Marks left in the soil along the Nile by . . . crocodiles."

"That's crazy! Can you imagine crocodiles

42

wandering up and down the high street?" Then Niall remembered the report he'd seen in the operations room of the Pyra-Base. "Hang on, though . . . CROCODILES PETRIFIED MY POOCH!"

"Quite so." Sam nodded. "It was said that many crocodiles were seen slithering into the sewers."

"But that was in London," Niall protested. "That's miles away."

He suddenly noticed a scrap of something fluttering at the back of one of the cages, and pulled it out. It felt strange — somehow *old*.

"That is papyrus," said Sam. "Ancient

43

Egyptian writing paper . . ."

The edges were burned, and mysterious squiggles were half visible through the blackened bits. "These symbols look a bit like hieroglyphs: Sam, what do they say?"

"They are like no hieroglyphs I have ever seen before." Sam looked baffled. "I cannot make face nor bottom of them!"

"Head nor tail, you mean," said Niall.

"OI!" A burly man had emerged through the broken back door and was pointing at Sam. "What are you doing in my garden, weirdo?"

Sam looked at Niall sadly. "He has spotted you."

"*Me*, a weirdo?" Niall spluttered, sticking the piece of papyrus in his pocket. "He's looking at—"

"Next time you must take disguise advice from me, my friend." Sam grinned and pressed his ribcage ruby. "But for now, we must fly!"

Niall saw the cattery owner's jaw drop

nearly to the floor as the ruby's red light flashed ... The garden faded from view, and for a moment Niall felt as though he was falling through deep, crimson custard ...

Sam and Niall landed on a doorstep outside a smaller house in a different street.

Suddenly, Niall found that *he* was wearing a sombrero and poncho too!

"What the heck?" he groaned.

46

"You look much better now, Niall." Sam had already rung the doorbell. "This is the house of Mr Hoyle – the man who found that Crystal of Ra in Giza. Cursed be those light-fingered burglars!"

The door opened and an old fellow with a suntan came out. He looked suspiciously at Sam and Niall in their fancy dress. Niall thanked his lucky stars that to anyone else but him, the grubby bandages would be invisible; they would see Sam as a normal human being. Or as normal as Sam ever got, anyway . . .

"Can I help you?" asked Mr Hoyle.

"No!" boomed Sam. "I have no need of assistance, old gentleman."

Niall stepped forward. "But we – that is, my, um, uncle and I – we would like to talk to you about your Egyptian souvenirs."

Mr Hoyle looked them up and down. "Are you from the holiday company?"

"We are excellent company, should you wish to go on holiday," Sam agreed.

The old man shook his head, confused, but then said, "You may as well come in. I was just brewing up." He ushered them into his small, untidy living room, then went into the kitchen

to make tea. "It happened when I was out in the shed, fetching some tools," he called out to them. "My hoover broke, you see. I'm trying to fix it."

Niall noticed a vacuum cleaner lying beside the sofa with its plastic cover off. Unable to resist the temptation to try and fix it, he picked it up and immediately delved into its workings.

"Anyway, while I was out, the burglars struck!" Mr Hoyle returned with three mugs of tea on a tray. "The funny thing is, they must've been wearing special shoes— Hey, what are you doing with my vacuum cleaner?"

"Just fiddling around." Niall grinned. "What do you mean, special shoes?"

Mr Hoyle shrugged. "Well, I haven't been able to clean up – you can still see the muddy footprints on the carpet . . ."

Sure enough, Niall could see the marks stretching across the floor, leading to a cabinet and back out to the front door. He gasped: "Sam, those prints look very familiar . . ."

Sam threw himself flat on the floor to inspect them. "Yes, my friend! They are the exact same

50

prints as those in the mud at the cattery!"

"Which means that Great Mew was right," Niall realized. "Whoever took the pussycats also stole the Crystal of Ra."

"Yes . . ." Sam stood up suddenly. "Thank you, old man, for your" – he looked down with a frown at the untouched mugs of tea – "for your strange brown liquid. We must now leave you in pieces. Please accept this special hat of apology." He thrust his sombrero onto the old man's head and rushed out of the house.

Niall hit the hoover's power switch, and it roared to life. "You can clean up the mess now,"

51

he said, and raised his own sombrero. "Bye!"

Leaving Mr Hoyle staring after him in amazement, Niall ran out to join Sam in the street. "So! Where to now?"

"Back to the Pyra-Base, my friend." Sam looked worried. "I have a most nasty suspicion of the danger we are facing. We must learn the truth of these strange hieroglyphs – and fast!"

Chapter Five

The Sinister Symbols

In very nearly no time at all, Sam and Niall had returned to the Pyra-Base. Sam's special ruby unlocked the pyramid's protective shield, and they landed back in the operations room.

A strange rasping, rumbling sound filled the air. Niall threw off his sombrero, instantly on guard. "What's that?"

"It is merely Great Mew!" Sam pointed to

the sphinx-shaped sofa: the snooty cat was curled up, snoring so loudly that her golden tiara rattled.

"Lazy old fish-bag," Niall muttered. "Skiving off while we do all the hard work . . ."

Sam put a bandaged finger to his equally bandaged lips, warning Niall to keep quiet – then tripped over an electrical cable and went crashing into the sofa.

"Help!" Great Mew meowed as she jerked awake, tiara flying, fur standing on end. "Police! Fire Brigade! Trout!"

"It's only us," Niall told her, as he

helped Sam to his feet.

Flustered, Mew turned her furious glance on the mummy. "You dare to disturb the sacred trance of Great Mew?"

"You were having a crafty kip!" Niall complained. "And while you were asleep, we found some clues. We need you to check them out."

He and Sam showed her the fragments of burned papyrus.

Trying to regain her dignity, Mew studied the scraps, her eyes growing slowly wider. "These sinister symbols . . ." Mew

shivered. "Can they really be . . . the Hieroglyphs of Horror?"

"That is my fear also, Great Mew," said Sam. "But I thought the hieroglyphs were just the ends of a ledge."

"Do you mean *legends*?" Niall felt a chill chipping at his spine. "What are Hieroglyphs of Horror?"

"Before I tell you, I must recover from this terrible shock." Mew eyed Sam beadily. "A small offering of fish might help."

"Of course, Great Mew," said Sam. "I shall smoke a herring at once."

Niall waited impatiently while Sam did the cooking. The second the fish was served, Mew pounced on the plate and nommed it down.

"Now . . . I shall tell you more." Mew lowered her voice to a dread whisper. "The Hieroglyphs of Horror are ancient spell-words with incredible power. They were formulated in the dark past by one of KaBa's most terrifying monsters: Sobek, known here on Earth as the crocodile-god."

"Crocodiles!" Niall gasped.

Sam quickly explained to Mew about the footprints they'd found.

"The TV news said that some animals went missing from Belfast Zoo," Sam recalled. "Perhaps the crocodiles escaped from there?"

Mew gave him a withering look. "Do you suppose they then flew from Northern Ireland to London, and then came here – to rob an old man?"

"Um, maybe," Sam persisted. "Perhaps they are, um, international master-criminal crocodiles of mystery!"

"Perhaps," said Niall loyally (but doubtfully). "Tell me, why was Sobek known as the Crocodile God?"

Mew pressed a button on her remote control, and an image appeared on the screen – a hunched, scaly figure with a hideous croc-like head.

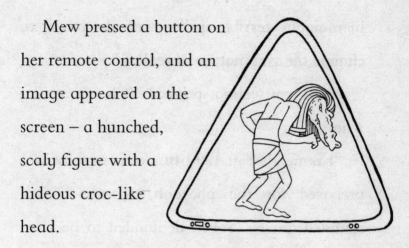

"Ask a silly question!" Niall gulped. "And what do these hieroglyphs do?"

"Once written on papyrus in a mystic ink, they can be sent great distances with a single breath," Mew told him. "And when the time is right, the papyrus burns, unleashing the

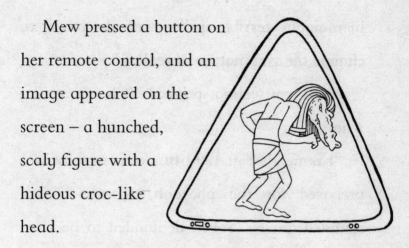

hieroglyphs' terrible spell – with the power to change the very nature of reality."

Niall was feeling spooked. "Change it into what?"

"I remember in 1290 BC, a great feast was prepared for the pharaoh, Ramses." Sam sounded grave. "Sobek demanded to be worshipped over all other gods; when Ramses refused, the feast was turned into maggots!" The mummy grimaced. "This was not so tasty."

"So many plump Nile fishies were lost. I wept for weeks!" Mew carefully turned the bits of papyrus over with the tips of her claws, as if

they might bite. "And that was just a warning. Sobek threatened to destroy all Egypt if he was not made Supreme Master of the World. That's why the other gods got together and destroyed him."

"So the story had a happy ending," said Niall. "But if Sobek's dead and gone, how come these hieroglyphs have turned up?"

"Perhaps someone has stolen Sobek's ancient powers," said Sam fearfully.

"And now they're using them to steal these Crystals of Ra . . ." Niall sighed. "If one crystal is strong enough to power the Pyra-Base's

energy shield, what could a whole load of crystals be used for?"

"*MEEEOW!* I shudder to think!" Mew went over to a pyramid-shaped machine. "That's why I have not been as idle as you suppose, boy . . . I have asked the techno-oracle to search the human world for any other crystals."

"Splendid!" Sam clapped. "Did you find the ones that were stolen?"

"Er, no. The thief must have them well hidden." Mew looked worried. "But it seems that there is just one more Crystal of Ra in the human world. It is kept in a private collection

of treasures, right . . . here."

She tapped a paw on the keyboard, and the image of an old, imposing house surrounded by fields appeared on the triangular screen.

"This is Gloveby House, in Scotland. Lord Gloveby has over a hundred Egyptian treasures in his collection – and right now he is abroad on business. The house stands empty! There is

nothing to stop our mystery robber stealing the crystal."

"Nothing . . . except us!" cried Sam. "If we take the crystal, the real robbers will have to come to *us* to get it!"

"Oh, yay!" said Niall sarcastically. "Sounds to me like whoever we're up against is pretty tough. Are you sure we can handle them?"

"We must take back-up." Sam stuck his bandaged fingers in his mouth and gave a loud whistle. "Mumbum! Here, boy!"

Niall smiled. Long ago, Mumbum had been Sam's police dog, but the poor hound had met

with a very nasty accident – only his bum remained intact! Sam had preserved Mumbum's rear end and rebuilt the rest of him, and the mummy-mutt had served him loyally ever since.

"Is he fully charged?" asked Niall.

Sam nodded. "And lucky for us, I prepared his heavy-duty action suit!"

There was a *whoosh!* from the corridor outside. Seconds later, a large steel nose like a gun-barrel poked into the room – quickly followed by bright-green shining

eyes, pointed ears, a chunky body with fiery jets shooting out of the paws, and all steered by a bandaged backside and tail. The tough, mostly-metallic dog-thing floated in, tail whizzing round like a propeller, and landed in front of Sam.

"Ahh!" Sam patted the dog's bottom, and the bandaged tail wagged happily. "Hello, brave Mumbum!"

Niall checked out the robo-hound. "I've not seen this suit before. He looks like a four-legged tank!"

"He is as tough as one too!" Sam held onto

Mumbum's ears, and Niall placed his hand on the dog-bot's back, ready to be transported – for longer magical journeys, the dog took the slog!

"While you are gone, I will study these hieroglyphs," Mew announced. "Perhaps the Rosetta Ray will shed some light on them."

Niall frowned. "The what?"

"It is a glorious machine," Sam revealed. "The Rosetta Ray can translate any language into any other language!"

"That would come in handy for French homework," said Niall. "Do you think this ray will work on supernatural squiggles?"

"The sooner you both leave, the sooner I can get on with finding out." The snooty cat bristled. "Be off with you!"

Niall rolled his eyes and Sam waved. "Now, Mumbum – take us to Scotland!"

Mumbum barked, his tail spinning. The world began to tilt and shake around Niall, shining silver as his sight went higgledy-piggledy. Suddenly he was falling through nothingness . . .

Chapter Six

Beware the McMummy!

WHUMP!

Niall and Sam and Mumbum were back on solid ground. They were standing in a large, shadowy room full of glass display cases. Thick curtains were drawn against the grey daylight. All was quiet, apart from the ticking of an old clock.

"We're trespassing," Niall whispered.

"What if we're caught?"

"Pardon?" boomed Sam.

"Shhhhh!" Niall hissed. "We've broken in, remember? Just like burglars!"

"Not so, my friend!" Sam cried. "We are non-burglars. *Anti*-burglars, to be welcomed by any homeowner!"

As he approached the curtains, Niall felt as if he was being watched. Peeping through the windows, he saw some cows in the neighbouring field, but no other signs of life. "Coast is clear. Shall we stick a light on?"

"No need. Behold!" Sam held up the index

finger of his left hand — and with a quiet *whoomph!* a small flame crackled from the end. "I call this Pharaoh's Fire!"

Niall grinned. "Just remember not to scratch your head."

Sam moved swiftly but silently from case to case, searching for the Crystal of Ra. "Aha!" He stopped near the corner of the room and beckoned to Niall.

"Phew," Niall whispered, as he saw a now familiar-looking stone behind glass, displayed on blue velvet. "The crystal's still there."

Sam blew out his finger. "Ready for *us* to

take into safe-keeping!"

But suddenly Mumbum started to growl, a low metallic sound followed by a loud *woof!*

"Shush, boy!" Niall whispered, his heart beginning to thump.

A scuttling, rustling sound was coming from behind the curtains.

Sam raised his bandaged fists. "Who is there?"

The curtains stirred – and then a loud, discordant wailing filled the air. Niall clutched his ears and gasped as a weird object – red and green and as big as a large dog – zoomed

towards him at terrifying speed . . .

Before he could react, his legs were knocked from under him and he crashed into a display case, banging his head. "OW!" As he dropped to the floor, out of the corner of his eye Niall glimpsed his mysterious attacker scuttling away into the shadows.

It looked like a red-checked shopping bag that had sprouted stick-like legs!

Mumbum growled and rose into the

air, ready to give
chase – when a long
strip of tartan
flipped over the top
of a nearby display
case, flew through the air and
struck him on the nose. There was a flash of
light, and the semi-mechanical hound froze in
mid-air.

The tartan strip fell to the floor, reared up
like a flattened, patterned snake and turned
towards Niall.

"What the heck is that?" Niall cried.

74

"I . . . I have not beheld such a thing for thousands of years!" Sam stared in amazement. "It is a wrap-worm — a weaponized bandage, used in the old days by certain Secret Agent Mummies. One touch will freeze you in time for up to five minutes."

"So that's what's happened to Mumbum!" Niall gulped as the wrap-worm edged closer. "Can't you stop it?"

"I shall try, my friend!" Sam darted forward and flicked a jet of Pharaoh's Fire from his left hand. *FWOOMPH!* The strip of fabric went up in smoke before it could do any more harm.

75

"Nice one, Sam." Niall looked about warily. "But don't forget, whatever knocked me over is still in this—"

"*HOOOTS!*" He was silenced by a mad shriek from behind him. "*Och aye, the nooooo!*"

In a blur of bandages, a bizarre figure shot out from behind a bookcase, and launched into a flying scissor-kick.

"OOOF!" Sam was struck in the chest and staggered backwards, slamming into the wall.

"Ha!" The attacking figure stood proudly, hands on hips. "Take *that* and shove it up yer haggis!"

Niall stared, astounded. Sam had been attacked by another *mummy*!

This mummy was shorter than Sam – and it seemed she was not so much Ancient Egyptian as Scottish. She wore a ragged, red-and-green

kilt, and many of her bandages were tartan too. On her head sat a battered red tam-o'-shanter with a threadbare pompom perched on the top. The wrappings on the mummy's face were daubed with blue stripes; she was like a bandaged Braveheart.

"Wait, foul thief!" Sam began. "Who are you?"

"I'm no thief – *you* are!" The female mummy spoke with a thick Scottish accent – almost like she was putting it on. "I'm yer worst nightmare, pal. Moira the McMummy, at your service!" Raising a fist, she hurled herself towards him . . .

Sam ducked under Moira's arm and pulled her hat down over her face. Then he tripped her up — but as she fell, she grabbed at his bandages, pulling him off balance. The two mummies crashed into a cabinet. Glass shattered and relics shot everywhere.

Niall scrambled up, ready to join the fight. But then the creepy shopping-bag-thing burst out of the gloom like a giant tartan tarantula and sped towards him. Niall jumped out of the way, onto the case containing the Crystal of Ra. *Whoosh!* The "bag" went hooting and honking past on its scurrying stick-legs,

79

knocking over another cabinet as it passed. The noise was excruciating!

"Away, hateful stealer of old relics!" cried Sam, driving back the McMummy with a barrage of ostrich-feather darts. One knocked the hat clean off her head. Moira was left reeling, and Sam pulled a small, pyramid-shaped object out from under his poncho. Niall recognized it as a pit-amid, and smiled. When Sam threw it to the floor and stamped on it, a hole would open up – big enough to capture a mad McMummy!

Sam raised his arm to throw the pit-amid –

80

but Moira just grinned. "Oh no ye don't, scally!" She groaned and strained – "GNNNNNN!" – and a heavy ostrich egg fell from her bandaged leg! She threw it at Sam's chest. Sam slipped, and the pit-amid flew backwards in an arc over his head . . .

THOMP! It struck the wall behind him. Immediately, a large triangular hole opened up, leading to the garden outside.

As Sam regained his balance and stared crossly at the hole, the shopping-bag-thing scuttled out of the shadows and raised what looked like a pipe from the top of its body.

"Look out, Sam!" Niall shouted. "It's aiming your way!"

ZAAAPP! A ray of green light shone from the pipe. Sam froze, teetered for a moment, then crumpled into a heap on the floor.

"Ha!" Moira the McMummy rubbed her bandaged hands together in glee and looked down at Sam. "Gotcha!"

Niall was still perched on the cabinet. "What have you done to my friend?"

The McMummy put her hands on her hips. "I've just stopped this scally from stealing a very special crystal."

"He wasn't trying to steal the Crystal of Ra for himself!" Niall hopped down and rushed to Sam's side; luckily he was still breathing. "He wanted to keep it safe from the real criminals, the ones we've been chasing—"

"But that was *my* plan!" Moira protested. "I tracked down the crystal – and sure enough, you came after it."

"No, we tracked the crystal, and *you* came after it. You and . . ." He frowned at the tartan bag with the pipe. "You and *that* weird thing."

"Dinna be so rude about poor wee Bogpipes!" said Moira, patting the bag-thing at her feet.

83

"Ye'll hurt his feelings."

"Bogpipes?" Niall peered at the creature in amazement. "Don't you mean '*bag*pipes'?"

"Och! Of course I mean Bogpipes. I made him myself." Moira nodded firmly. "Now watch your mouth. Bogpipes shot your mummy friend with his stun-pipe, and he can shoot you too if I want him to."

Sure enough, the strange bag-creature scuttled over with a shrill, wailing noise and stopped in front of Niall, waving its stun-pipe menacingly.

"There's no need for that," Niall said quickly.

84

"As for this big lump . . ." Moira scowled at Sam. "He frazzled my poor wee wrap-worm to dust! I ought to do the same to him—"

"No!" Sam's eyes opened, and he stared at Moira in wonder. "I remember you."

"Do ye?" She stared back. "Hmmm . . . Now that ye mention it, yon bandages do look familiar . . ."

"You are a Secret Agent Mummy, just like me." Sam looked delighted. "I thought I was the last of my kind."

"Aye, me too." Moira smiled. "Well, hang out the sporrans, now there are two of us!"

 85

Sam's grin could've lit the room. "Did you stay here on Earth to catch criminals from KaBa, as I did?"

"No, I did not!" she informed him. "I just like the scenery on Earth, ye ken? And the best is to be found right here in bonnie Scotland. I've been here for a thousand years!" She smiled proudly. "I'm proper Scottish the noo!"

"No one Scottish really talks like that, though," Niall said.

"Och aye, ye ken the misty glen o' the loch, hootenanny!" Moira shot back. "Now come on, admit it – ye stole those Crystals of Ra, didn't ye? And ye came here for this one too."

"No." Sam shook his head. "We are not to blame."

87

"Right," said Niall. "And if you're not to blame either, Moira . . . who is?"

"Hmmm. Perhaps we're on the same side after all." She stuck out her hand and helped Sam to his feet. "Well, I s'pose we'd better swap notes and work together."

"Hooray!" Sam beamed at Niall. "We have an ally!"

Niall nodded. "I'd sooner have her as a friend than an enemy!"

Just then, Mumbum jerked back to life as the wrap-worm's time-freeze wore off. He dropped to the ground, marched up to Bogpipes, took a

quick sniff with his gun-barrel nose, and then gave a low, warning growl.

Moira scowled. "Could ye ask your doggie to stop growling at my poor wee Bogpipes?"

"It is all right, boy," Sam told Mumbum.

The robo-dog clanked closer to Bogpipes and growled again. It was then Niall realized that Mumbum was looking *past* Moira's piping pet – out through the triangular hole in the wall. The field was clearly visible outside, but all the cows had disappeared . . .

A scrap of scorched papyrus blew in from outside, marked with the familiar symbols.

 89

"The Hieroglyphs of Horror! Here!" Niall suddenly felt icy cold. "Uh-oh . . ."

Everyone jumped as a huge dark snout pushed into the room through the hole in the wall.

"Look out!" Sam shouted.

Mumbum woofed in warning as a rampaging reptile with red, glowing eyes slithered into the room. It was as big as a sofa and hard as rock. Niall stared, horrified: it was followed by another four similar monsters.

"Crocodiles," he breathed.

Scaly tails slapping the floor, huge jaws bristling with teeth, the mutant crocs crept closer.

Chapter Seven

Action off the Scales!

"Yon crocs are not like any I've ever seen before," said Moira, backing away. "What are they doing here?"

Sam gulped. "They are either going to steal the crystal . . . or eat us for dinner."

"Or both," Niall added.

"Eat? Steal? Huh!" Moira tutted. "I'm not taking this lying down!"

"That is because you are standing up,

Moira!" said Sam reasonably.

The five mutant crocs bared their teeth as they approached.

Sam looked down at Mumbum. "Attack, boy. Attack!"

"Get them, laddie!" cried Moira, at the same time.

Mumbum barked, and Bogpipes gave a loud, off-key toot.

With a crack like cannon fire, smoky green bullets burst from Mumbum's nose-gun, exploding over the creepy crocs. Bogpipes fired his stun-ray – but neither attack worked. The

crocs kept up their relentless advance, hissing with excitement. Niall, Sam and Moira were forced back against the far wall.

"Those are some tough handbags-in-training," Moira observed.

Niall pointed to the first croc-creature, which had slunk away from the others. "That one's up to something!"

Sure enough, the monster was darting towards the case containing the Crystal of Ra; it smashed it open with one flick of its deadly tail.

"Leave this to me!" shouted Sam.

"I've got this covered!" cried Moira.

Sam and Moira both leaped over the four snapping crocs at the same time, grabbing some serious air – at least, until they collided and

collapsed in a heap on top of a bookcase, squashing it flat. Niall wished he could jump out of reach of the crocodile monsters – but they had turned, as one, to follow Sam and Moira, who now were struggling to their feet.

"Sam! Moira!" Niall shouted his warning. "They're after you!"

Mumbum and Bogpipes resumed their attack – Sam's flying dog dive-bombing from above, and Moira's preternatural pipe-bag sticking stun-bolts up the crocs' butts. The indestructible creatures barely seemed to notice. In desperation, Niall hurled heavy books at them. They

simply bounced off the monsters' hard hides.

"Leave this to me!" Moira shouted as the first of the crocs crawled towards the crystal. She ripped off a strip of bandage and pointed at the croc, incanting magical words as she did so:

Hear me, elements!
My desire
Is to conjure up
A wall of fire!

All at once, a wall of flame sprang up between the croc and the shattered case!

 97

Unfortunately, as Moira was casting her spell, Sam flicked his wrist and sent out a shower of sand. It quickly turned into a whirling sand-storm so powerful that it immediately put out Moira's wall of flame – turning it into molten mush as it did so.

The other four crocs were closing in fast, and Moira and Sam had to jump away again. Meanwhile the first mutant monster slithered slyly through the black remains of the sand.

"No!" cried Niall as at last the croc's jaws closed on the Crystal of Ra. "We've got to get it back!"

Sam dived at the croc — but it spun round with surprising speed and swatted him with its tail. He tumbled backwards into Moira — and again the pair fell in a heap.

It was up to Niall to retrieve the crystal: he looked around for something he could use to prise open the croc's jaws — some splintered wood, perhaps, or a poker — but there was nothing to hand. With the special stone securely in its chops, the creature turned and slithered back through the hole in the wall. The four guard crocs snarled viciously at Mumbum and Bogpipes before lumbering after their leader.

"Come!" cried Sam, helping Moira to her feet. "There is still time to rescue the crystal!" The mummies ran for the hole and scrambled through. Niall chased after them with Mumbum and Bogpipes – just in time to see a line of croc-creatures departing through an open man- hole in the driveway, vanishing into the sewers beneath.

"Och, we canna tell them apart," Moira cried. "We'll never find the one with the Crystal of Ra now!"

Niall frowned. "Where *did* they all come from?"

"I do not know, my friend," said Sam, staring around. "But look, the cows have gone from the fields."

"Aye," Moira agreed. "Those wicked crocs must've chomped their way through the lot of them."

"We're lucky they didn't chomp their way through *us*." Niall shuddered.

101

"Remain still, evil magic crocodiles!" Sam commanded, to no avail. "Cursed be your sharp teeth, impregnable hides and similar appearance!"

But the last of the scaly brutes *did* stop. It opened its jaws to reveal a small scroll of papyrus, and spat it towards them.

Niall recognized the ink on the paper in a heartbeat. "Hieroglyphs of Horror!" he shouted. "Incoming!"

But Mumbum bravely flew up and caught the scroll in his mechanical jaws. His mouth closed tight, sealing it inside, and he landed

with his tail wagging. The crocodile eyed him nastily, then slid down into the sewers after its fellows.

"Get back here, croc!" bellowed Moira and jumped down the manhole. Sam dived in too. Niall jumped onto Mumbum's back and rode into the smelly darkness after them.

Sam was peering around in the light of the Pharaoh's Fire which flared from his finger. The sewer tunnels stretched out in seven different directions.

"Och, we've lost them!" Moira glared at Sam. "Thanks to you, those monsters got clean

103

away with the crystal!"

"I would have stopped them with my super-sandstorm if you had not interfered with your silly wall of flame!" he replied crossly. "You should be most grateful! Mumbum saved us from those Hieroglyphs of Horror. What did your big boggy bagpipes do?"

"We don't need help from a bandaged bum with a tin can stuck to it," Moira retorted.

Still keeping his metal mouth shut, Mumbum gave a muffled woof.

"Guys, arguing isn't going to help anything," Niall broke in. "Say you're sorry."

Sam and Moira looked at each other but said nothing.

"I mean it!" he said sternly. "We've got to work together."

"I s'pose we do," Moira muttered. Sam nodded and offered his hand. The McMummy took it.

"Good." Niall breathed a sigh of relief. "Now, is there a chance we can track the crystal before those crocodiles take it back to their master?"

"Och, it's worth a try," Moira replied. "My Pyra-Base is closest."

Sam clapped his hands together. "Let us go!"

Mumbum lifted Niall back up to the driveway, where Bogpipes was waiting. Moira and Sam joined them a few moments later.

"Hang on." Niall looked at the hole in the wall of the house. "Lord Gloveby won't be too happy when he gets back to find this mess."

"It's nothing a Spell of Putting Right won't fix." Moira pointed at the room and bellowed:

Boom, bam, bonk, kapow!
Put the room right,
and put it right NOW!

In a flash of distinctly tartan lightning, the wall was repaired. Niall rushed to the window and saw that the room inside was just as it had been when they'd first arrived; only now the Crystal of Ra was missing. A blackened scrap of papyrus blew around his feet. He picked it up and stuck it in his pocket.

"Your magic is strong, Moira," said Sam, impressed.

107

"Aye, well, I've been storing it up these past few centuries." She picked up Bogpipes and started to squeeze and pump him like a set of tartan bellows. "C'mon, let's get a shift on." A drunken-sounding whine started up from the piping pet, and an orange glow filled the air.

"Here we go again," Niall breathed. "Only this time by magic bagpipe power!"

"Away we gooooooo!" Moira shouted, pumping her pet faster. The light grew brighter and the band of extraordinary figures faded from view.

Lord Gloveby's hall stood in gloomy silence once again . . . or, almost in gloomy silence.

Had anyone remained outside the house, and had they been listening very carefully, they might have caught the sound of low, mocking laughter drifting up from the sewers below . . .

Chapter Eight

The Sting of the Symbols

The journey to Moira's Pyra-Base was swift. It was a pyramid, pretty much like Sam's, only in the middle of a field of heather, overlooking a beautiful loch. The ancient paintings on the walls of the entrance hall had been embellished so that the towering figures now wore tam-o'-shanters and bright tartan sashes and kilts.

"Follow me!" Moira led the way to her

operations room. Unlike Sam's, it was lit by electric light, and had a lot less weird tech and bric-a-brac. Stuffed Egyptian animals stood around the room – a hippo, a jackal, a goat, a scarab beetle . . .

"AAAARGH!" Niall shouted suddenly.

A crocodile perched on the table.

"Och, don't fret, laddie. It's just a stuffed souvenir, like all the others." Moira petted it fondly. "Used to see a lot of these on the banks of the Nile."

"Lovely." Niall sat beside Sam on a tartan-covered couch. Mumbum hovered obediently by Sam's feet, one robotic eye fixed on Bogpipes. The tooting terror had taken up position on the other side of the room, but was keeping a close watch on Mumbum.

"Right, let's check for any sign of the crystal on my techno-oracle . . ." Moira fiddled with some buttons on a gleaming silver pyramid.

Niall felt uneasy. "Moira, what if those crocs come after us again? Do you have any security here?"

"Besides Bogpipes, ye mean?" She pointed to a small stone pyramid flashing in the corner. "I have these special 'aye-spy' cameras about the place." She pressed a stone button and a big triangular wall-screen blinked on. It was split into six segments, with different views of the rooms in Moira's Pyra-Base. Niall saw images of the main entrance hall with its ancient wall paintings, a number of corridors, the operations room they stood in and a stable full of camels

113

shifting
in their
stalls.

"Ah!" Sam smiled. "Though you are no longer an active Secret Agent Mummy, you still have your magic camels!"

"Of course! Where else would I get the milk for my porridge?" Suddenly Moira grabbed a couple of sticky bowls from a table. "While we're waiting for yon techno-oracle, let's have some porridge goodness, aye?" Into each of them she ladled some thick white goo from a

cauldron, adding four spoonfuls of salt. She slapped the bowls down in front of Niall and Sam.

"Er, no thanks," said Niall.

"EAT IT AND SHUT UP!" boomed Moira.

He gingerly tried a salty spoonful, almost threw up, and passed his bowl to Sam, who ate the whole lot as well as his own in just a few seconds.

"So delicious!" He turned to Mumbum. "Do you wish for some, boy?"

Mumbum shook his head as a strip of ticker

115

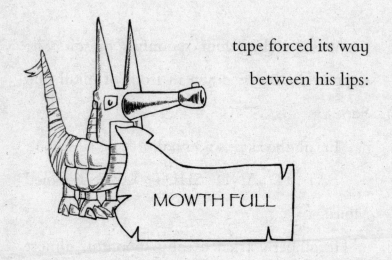

tape forced its way
between his lips:

MOWTH FULL

He's still got that piece of papyrus with the hieroglyphs on, Niall realized.

A downcast *BLOOP* from the techno-oracle signalled that the search for the crystal had ended badly. "Och, pants!" Moira growled. "Not a sign of it!"

"It has vanished like all the others," Sam agreed sadly.

"Hmmm . . ." Niall pulled the piece of blackened papyrus he'd found at Lord Gloveby's out of his pocket. "I wonder why these hiero-glyphs burned up, while the ones in Mumbum's mouth didn't?"

"Perhaps because there is no air in his metal mouth," Sam suggested. "Without air, fires cannot start!"

"That must be it." Niall smiled. "Which means that now we have a scroll with a *complete* spell on it. Mumbum, can you give us a printout

of those hieroglyphs – like a photocopy?"

"Of course, my friend. All his body-suits have a built-in tum-scanner!" Sam beamed. "The copy will be ready in five minutes – eh, Mumbum?"

The robo-dog gave a muffled woof, gulped and nodded. His tummy began to rattle and hum as his scanner switched on.

"Once we have the copy, we can show it to Mew," said Niall. "She can use the Rosetta Ray to translate it."

"If we learn what the hieroglyphs do," said Sam, "we may find a way to stop them!"

118

"Wait. Mew? *Great* Mew?" Moira stuck out her tongue. "I remember that fish-munching moggy. It was her sort that made me want to retire in the first place."

Niall grinned – he knew where Moira was coming from! "But if you're retired, how come you came to Lord Gloveby's looking for the crystal thief?"

"Because the thief took *my* crystal, the scally. If I caught him, I could make him give it back!" Moira sat down crossly. "Then I could switch my shield on again and enjoy my retirement in peace and quiet."

119

"I wish I was knowing why this mystery thief wants so many crystals," said Sam.

"Och, everyone collects something!" Moira shrugged. "Like, I collect recipes for Scotch broth."

"Broth!" Sam cried. "But, Moira, you are a Secret Agent Mummy! How could you choose cooking a filling soup over hooking a super-villain?"

"Easy!" said Moira. "Och, the job was all right for the first thousand years. But honestly – guarding pharaohs who couldn't even tinkle without wanting a song written about it? It got

on my nerves!" She shivered. "Then I got in a battle with a wizard called Azmal Sekra."

Niall gasped. "We met him!"

"And got rid of him!" Sam added proudly.

"GOOD!" Moira exclaimed. "I battled against him at Abu Simbel, and he magicked me into the heart of a mountain. Took me a couple of centuries to dig myself out. And by then, everyone from KaBa had pushed off." She glanced at Sam. "Or so I thought. Anyway, since then I've lived the quiet life with only Bogpipes and my sweet, wee camels for company."

121

BING! Mumbum chimed, and a strip of coloured paper curled out of his snout.

"The copy is ready!" Sam snatched it from Mumbum and patted him on the head. "Moira, may we let Great Mew know of our discovery?"

"Aye, I suppose ye can talk to her over the video-screen," Moira grumbled. "Ye ken how it works?"

"Of course. But who is Ken?"

"Och, just get on with it!"

While Sam typed his Pyra-Base address into a computer keyboard, Niall looked at the

spooky hieroglyphs. Some looked like weird monsters, others like blue wounds slashed into the paper. A feeling of foreboding tingled through him.

One of the screens on the wall glowed green. Moments later it showed Mew with a fishtail hanging from her mouth. She

123

was sitting beside a sort of stone telescope with a triangular lens. It was attached to a big monitor, computer and keyboard, all of which were made of jade.

So that's the Rosetta Ray, thought Niall.

"MEEEOWWWWW!" Mew glanced up at the screen. "Mummy? How can you be calling me? That cannot be another Pyra-Base—?"

"It IS, the noo!" Moira barged in front of the screen. "So shut yer fish-trap!"

"Eek! Another mummy!" The cat looked aghast, then recovered. "Have you come to

124

worship Great Mew?"

"Worship a great windy pain in the sporran, ye mean? No!" Moira held up Mumbum's photocopy. "Now, shut up and point your Rosetta Ray at this printout."

Mew's eyes widened and she licked her lips. "A prim trout?"

Sam quickly bundled Moira aside before she exploded. "A printout, Great Mew, of a complete spell written in the Hieroglyphs of Horror!"

"*What?*" said Mew. "Whatever has been going on?"

 125

Sam quickly brought her up to speed on their adventures.

"You have done quite well," said Mew, at last. "All the Rosetta Ray has told me so far is that the spell-scrap you found was not written in ink . . . but in blood."

"Blood?" Niall echoed. "But it's blue."

"Blue is the colour of gods' blood on KaBa." Mew preened. "Naturally, I too have blue blood."

"I should've known!" Niall frowned. "So we're definitely dealing with a god. A god who controls crocodiles."

"Och, Sobek is dead, I tell you!" Moira cried.

Mew agreed: "The gods who destroyed him checked his body for signs of life. There were none."

Sam looked grave. "Perhaps the printout will give us a clue as to who wrote these new hieroglyphs?"

"Perhaps." Mew crossed to the controls of the stone telescope. "Hold it up, boy!"

Niall held up the printout, and Mew switched on the machine. The parchment was bathed in green light.

"It's analysing the writing . . ." Mew sighed. "No good. The meaning is unknown. Except for this symbol at the top . . . which says, TIME DELAY."

Niall gulped. "Time delay?"

"*WOOF!*"

At the urgent bark, Niall turned – to find that Mumbum was starting to shake. A spooky glow shone from inside his mouth. *PTAH!* He spat out the papyrus,

which had started to smoke.

"The spell," cried Sam. "It has been activated!"

Moira groaned. "Set to go off on a time delay!"

"The croc who spat it at us must have *wanted* Mumbum to grab it," Niall realized. "So it would go off later – here in your Pyra-Base!"

As the papyrus blackened, smoke swirled upwards and a supernatural breeze started up. Strange symbols and hieroglyphs began to form in mid-air. Mumbum barked, and Bogpipes tooted hard; the symbols were swooping and

buzzing about the room like wasps at a picnic.

"Don't let them touch you!" Mew commanded from the screen, as Sam, Niall and Moira huddled together. "The Rosetta Ray is working now! There are letters forming . . . words . . ."

Something else was forming too, before Niall's horrified eyes. As the hieroglyphs spun about, they traced a glowing image.

The image of a hideous creature with a man's body and the brutal head of a crocodile.

Mew squeaked with fear as she read aloud: "SOBEK HAS YOU NOW . . ."

Chapter Nine

The Enemy Within

"Sobek!" Sam swiped at the symbols shimmering around him. "Then . . . he really *is* behind the hieroglyphs!"

"Sure explains the crocs!" Niall shouted, hiding under a table.

"SOBEK BRINGS CHANGE." Mew was still reading aloud. "SOBEK, MASTER OF MATTER . . ."

"But Sobek was destroyed by the other gods," groaned Moira. "Gods don't make mistakes . . ."

The sinister wind blew more fiercely still. Mumbum rose into the air and fired his nose-blaster, barking and snapping his jaws at the smoking symbols. Bogpipes tried to join in too, zapping the symbols with his stun-ray. He hit several of the stuffed animals that decorated the room, then – *BLAMM!* – a stray blast struck the screen showing Great Mew. It blew apart.

Finally the last of the symbols drifted up from the blackened parchment and swept

through the open door, out of the operations room. Mumbum and Bogpipes dropped down beside their respective owners, awaiting instructions.

Niall crawled out from under the table. "Where did the hieroglyphs go?"

"I do not know." Sam looked more worried than Niall had ever seen him. "Evil hieroglyphs made from the blood of an evil god . . . We must see where they went."

"Perhaps they just blew away?" said Niall hopefully.

"Aye. And a wee piggy just flew out from

my kilt." Moira jumped up and checked the aye-spy cams. Luckily, the other scanner screens were still working.

The view of the stables caught Niall's eye. The camels were restless, shuffling and stamping about. Their grunts filled the air, as did certain smoky symbols . . .

"Look!" Sam pointed.

"Och, not in the stables . . ." Moira pressed some buttons to zoom in on the scene – in time to catch a camel's lips close around the last of the smoky hieroglyphs. "Oh, WHAT?"

"The camels have *eaten* the hieroglyphs!"

135

Sam cheered. "That is one way to deal with them. Praised be their brave if unusual appetites!"

"I don't think they should have done that," Niall murmured. Was it something to do with the screen, or were Moira's camels turning *green*? He watched, appalled, as their furry hides turned scaly. Their humps were shrinking, as were their

136

legs, and their mouths were growing longer, pointier . . .

Moira boggled at the screen. "They . . . they're turning into crocodiles!"

Sobek brings change . . . Niall remembered the words on the screen. "Do you think that's what happened to the cats in the cattery, the zoo animals—?"

"And the cows in the fields at Gloveby House!" Sam bit his bandaged fingernails. "The hieroglyphs changed them all into crocodile monsters – under Sobek's control."

"I've got to save my camels!" yelled Moira

in anguish. With a swish of tartan she was out of the door, before anyone could say a word. Bogpipes gave a valiant "toot" and scuttled after his mistress.

"She will need our help," Sam declared. "Come!"

Mumbum gave a quiet woof, fired his paw jets, and weaved a somewhat wobbly path after him. Frowning, Niall followed him. "You OK, boy?"

The robo-dog waved his bandaged tail weakly, and kept on flying. Niall ran as fast as he could, and found that he was

leaving Mumbum behind.

"The stables must be down here," Sam panted. He took a corner at speed – and almost immediately skidded to a halt beside Moira, who had stopped dead.

Niall slid to a standstill just behind them both. At the end of the corridor he could see a huge, empty stable – there were no camels . . .

All the camels were crocodiles now.

Twenty mutant crocodiles, crawling out of their stalls to block the corridor completely. They glared at Niall, Sam, Moira and Bogpipes with cold crimson eyes.

Niall felt sick with terror. The crocs dragged their monstrous green bellies across the stone floor, advancing fast. Bogpipes fired tartan rays at the reptiles, but again, his attack had little effect.

"It's no good!" shouted Moira. "Run for it!"

"We still have Mumbum!" Sam cried. "Boy! Where are you?"

There was a sound of misfiring jets behind them. Niall felt a surge of relief – until he saw the robo-dog.

Mumbum's eyes were glowing red. And while his metal suit was just the same, the

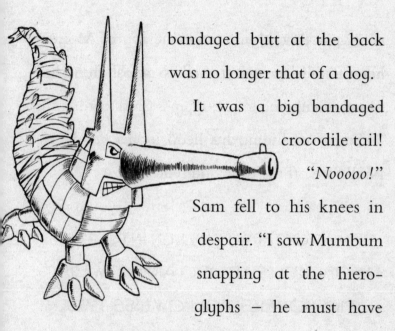

bandaged butt at the back was no longer that of a dog.

It was a big bandaged crocodile tail!

"*Nooooo!*"

Sam fell to his knees in despair. "I saw Mumbum snapping at the hiero-glyphs – he must have swallowed one too!"

"Let us pass, Mumbum?" Niall begged him. "Please?"

Mumbum fired a warning shot from his

nose-gun that almost took the top of Moira's hat off. Tickertape started to spool from his metal mouth.

Sam was hiding his head in his hands, so Niall tore off the tape and read it:

YOO HAV FAWLLEN INTO
SOBEK'S TRAP. YOO ARE NOW HIS
PRISSONERS. FOLLOW USS TWO
SOBEK'S LAIR OR DIE.

The croc-monster at the front of the pack glared at Niall, Sam and Moira and bared its

142

teeth in warning, its huge tail flicking from side to side. It scuttled forward, and its meaning was clear: it was time to move.

Moira looked at Niall and Sam, and sighed. "What a rubbish day *this* is turning out to be!"

Chapter Ten

In the Lair of Sobek

Sam, Niall, Moira and Bogpipes were herded by the crocodiles out of the McMummy's Pyra-Base and into the field of heather. Mumbum, his bandaged croco-butt twitching unpleasantly, led the way towards the loch. Niall had never seen Sam look so worried, and felt very sad himself. It was awful to see the plucky dog's-bottom-bot transformed into something so horrid.

"Sobek is up to something big," Sam muttered. "I can feel it in my preserving fluids."

Niall nodded. "He's been collecting Crystals of Ra. Each time he tracks one down, he uses the Hieroglyphs of Horror to transform a local bunch of animals into crocodile-slaves who can steal it for him."

"Och, but why does he *want* so many crystals?" Moira growled.

"I fear we may soon be finding out," said Sam.

Mumbum paused at the edge of the dark loch. The waters bubbled and parted to create a

clear corridor down to the sandy, silty bed. Behind them, the crocodiles hissed and snapped, driving them forward.

Niall shivered as he stumbled between the surging waters, which seemed held back by invisible walls.

"Projected energy," Moira observed. "Sobek is using his Crystals of Ra to push power through space."

Just then a strange noise sounded from the field of heather – a noise like gongs clanging, drums rattling and a choir of wailing giants singing sea shanties.

Niall glanced back – and gasped at the sight of Sam's Pyra-Base blurring into being beside Moira's.

"Great Mew!" Sam breathed.

"Bogpipes blew up the video-link," Niall remembered. "Mew must have brought the

147

Pyra-Base here to find out what happened."

Sam nodded. "Let us hope she sees our predicament and runs away at once, never risking her glorious life to help us."

"*I'm* not hoping for that!" Niall protested.

"Och, of course she won't help us!" said Moira. "I'm sure the scraggy wee pain will moan that there's no one to cook fish for her and push off home again."

With a grating noise, a stone hatchway in the loch bed slowly opened to receive them. Bogpipes produced a trembling wail and tried to run back to shore, but Mumbum blasted him,

148

and a swirl of smoke burst from the tartan airbag.

"Watch what you're doing!" Moira snapped.

The robo-dog knocked her to the ground. Tickertape chuntered from his mouth, which read:

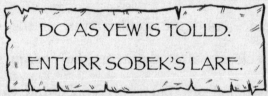

DO AS YEW IS TOLLD.

ENTURR SOBEK'S LARE.

The crocodile monsters snapped and hissed, waving their tails.

"Guess we have no choice," said Niall quietly.

149

He followed Sam and Moira through the hatch and into a sloping tunnel. Shallow steps had been carved into the side. It was dark and dank and cold; the flaming torches set into the walls gave little light and no heat at all. Niall heard the grating of the stone hatch as it slid back into place, and the sudden rush of the loch's waters closing over them, as the energy shield was switched off. Then the only sound was the cold scrunch and scrape of creeping crocodiles, the dank drip of water on stone and Mumbum's jets as he kept bumping into them to keep them moving. Swiping his horrible tail, he herded them

towards a golden light at the end of the tunnel.

A snarling growl rang out: "Let the prisoners approach!"

"Please can I go to the toilet?" Sam asked brightly, hoping to make a polite exit.

But there was no escape. Mumbum and the crocodiles pushed their prisoners into a large sandstone chamber. With the TV screens and charts and huge stone jars, it reminded Niall of Sam's operations room, but with one major difference: this space was dominated by a vast stone throne, its edges covered in fearsome spikes.

151

Crocodile teeth! Niall realized.

And upon the throne sat a huge, bloated figure.

It had the body of a muscular man, wrapped in sheets of beaten gold and wearing silver sandals. But it was the cruel reptilian head that caught Niall's attention. The thick, scaly

jaws were dark green; the nostrils twitched and flared with each heavy breath; eyes as big as oranges and bright as naked flames glared down at him. Niall wanted to run away screaming, but the hungry-looking crocs behind him kept him rooted to the spot.

"Welcome, foolish ones," rumbled the figure on the throne. "I am Sobek."

"Greetings, darkest lord!" Sam bowed low. "We had not thought to meet you, thinking you dead for the last three thousand years."

"What have ye been doing all this time?" Moira demanded, wiping a bandaged finger

through the dust on a canopic jar. "'Cos it sure as heck wasn't the cleaning."

"I have been surviving." Sobek watched her coldly. "My fellow gods thought they'd destroyed me. But the Hieroglyphs of Horror saved me. The symbols' magic made it appear as though I *was* dead — when in fact I was merely in a healing trance."

"Clever," said Moira.

Sobek nodded. "When I recovered, thousands of years later, I found that my Pyra-Base was dead. The power in my Crystal of Ra had run out."

154

"So you stole other crystals," Sam guessed.

"I?" Sobek roared. "I, God of Crocodiles, go out and steal like a common criminal?" He shook his horrible head and snapped his jaws shut. "Never."

"The crocs," Niall breathed. "They're your servants. You sent *them* out to steal for you, didn't you?"

"Of course I did." Sobek sat back down on the throne. "When they went back to KaBa, my godly brothers and sisters left many Crystals of Ra behind in Ancient Egypt. My crocodiles gathered all they could find, but still I needed

 155

more. I fixed my Pyra-Base and travelled the Earth, hunting down all the others."

"But many lands have no crocodiles," Sam realized. "So you used the Hieroglyphs of Horror to turn ordinary animals into super-crocs to fetch and carry for you."

"Correct." Sobek gave a toothy, terrible smile. "As you have observed, the Hieroglyphs of Horror can transform living creatures."

"Aye, very nice." Moira shuddered. "Well, ye came here and pinched my crystal. How many are left?"

"Just one." Sobek leered at Sam. "*Yours*. I'm

glad your cat-goddess has brought your Pyra-Base to my doorstep. It makes taking the final Crystal of Ra so much simpler."

Sam sighed. "Great Mew will not be able to defend herself from attacking crocodiles."

"She will not have to." Sobek laughed. "My Hieroglyphs of Horror will transform *her* into my willing croco-slave!" He raised a fist. "She will put the crystal right here in my hand."

"Poor Great Mew!" Sam muttered.

"Why do you need so many crystals, Sobek?" Niall demanded.

"Because, gathered together, their power

will make me invincible," said Sobek. "I do not need machines to control the crystals, as these mummies do to shield their pyramids. As a god, I control the crystals' energy using only my mind!" He turned to Niall. "Shall I demonstrate?"

His eyes glowed . . .

And suddenly Niall was pushed back against the wall by a glowing yellow bubble. "Hey!"

"You see? I can conjure a shield and control it, just with my thoughts! That is how I parted the waters up above – by projecting the crystals' power with my mind." Sobek nodded, pleased

with himself. "But that is a mere conjuring trick. I mean to use the crystals for something far more . . . spectacular."

Moira glowered at him. "It's got something to do with the hieroglyphs, hasn't it?"

"Correct." Sobek stared back at her until she was forced to look away. "Do you know how I deliver my hieroglyph spells to their destination?"

Sam nodded. "It was said in the old time that you blew them with a single breath."

"Yes, indeed. Though I could send them no further than a few hundred earthly miles."

159

Sobek's drooling jaws cranked open in a grin. "However, over the long centuries of hiding here, I have learned how to increase the range of my spells – by marrying the magic of the hieroglyphs with the power of the crystals."

"You have married them?" Sam scratched his head. "I hope the weather was nice! Was there cake?"

"Cease your prattle!" Sobek boomed. He jumped up from his throne, pounded across the stone floor and pulled on an ebony lever set into the wall. A panel slowly rose up to reveal a chamber bathed in a burning orange light

160

– Crystals of Ra, too many to count, were piled up in a kind of shining pyramid – with a space at the top for just one more. "The more crystals I have, the greater the distance my evil spells can travel. I need only *one* more . . . then I will have enough to project the Hieroglyphs of Horror thousands and thousands of miles . . . ALL AROUND THE EARTH."

Moira's bandages had turned pale. "You mean . . . you'll be able to change every single

161

animal on the planet into yon monster crocodiles?"

"Yes! Billions and billions of them!" Sobek gave a thick, throaty laugh. "They shall attack and *eat* humankind at my command."

"No!" Niall shouted. "Your crocs can't eat everyone."

"Of course they can!" Sobek retorted. "Land animals alone outnumber humans by eight to one!"

"But we have armies and navies and air forces," Niall protested. "Humans will find you, and get you!"

"I shall be quite safe here behind my own personal energy shield," Sobek gloated, "until the last soldier is swallowed. *Then* I shall rise and rule the Earth!"

"A planet of crocodiles," said Sam, "eating everything in their path . . ."

Sobek's body rocked with laughter. "As for you, you mummified relics, it would please me to have you serve mighty Sobek, as you would have served the pharaohs in the old time."

"No way!" said Moira hotly.

"If you refuse . . . the boy here will die." Sobek laughed and snapped his jaws, his dark

scales aglow in the light of the crystals. "With the power of the hieroglyphs and the crystals in my claws, my supremacy is absolute. After so long spent hiding in the dark . . . the whole world shall belong to Sobek!"

Chapter Eleven

Grave and Watery!

Sam stepped towards Sobek and fell to his knees. "Of course we shall serve you, O Mighty One."

Niall couldn't believe his ears. "Huh?"

"What're ye on aboot?" Moira cried.

"You and I, Moira – we shall serve Sobek!" He winked frantically at the McMummy. "Shan't we?"

Moira looked blank. "Have ye got

165

something in your eye?"

"No!" Sam was speaking through gritted teeth now. "I am just saying, of *course* we shall serve Sobek! Yes?"

Sobek's huge eyes were focused on him. "What trickery is this?"

"I mean it!" Sam got to his feet. "Tell me, Sobek, how may I serve you? A drink of water, perhaps?" Suddenly he unplugged his palm and a huge spray of water burst from his bandages. "Here – have a delta force blast in your face!"

"FOOL!" At once, Sobek's bubble of energy appeared around his scaly body, and the water

splattered harmlessly off. "Did you think such a pathetic trick would work?"

"I did a bit," Sam admitted.

"It might still work on your wee friends!" Moira spun round, pulled the bung from her own bandaged palm and also fired a delta force blast. *SWOOOOSH!* It came out like a tidal wave. The monster crocs were swept away in a foaming tide, smashing into urns and crashing against the walls.

"Now, laddie!" Moira grabbed Niall by the scruff of the neck and practically hurled him from Sobek's lair. "Run for it!"

He hovered in the doorway. "I can't leave you!"

"Warn Great Mew, my friend!" Sam shouted. "She must take the Pyra-Base away from here. Sobek MUST NOT get the final crystal – or the human world is doomed!"

"You mummies cannot defy me!" Safe behind his shield, the croc-god snapped his fingers. Mumbum – his paw-jets propelling him above the flood – flew straight at Moira,

his gun ready to fire . . .

But Bogpipes jumped up under him, knocking him aside. Mumbum fired over Moira's head.

"Mumbum, *fetch*!" With a magical flick of his bandaged sleeve, Sam produced a huge ostrich egg and threw it at the robo-dog's metal face. The egg cracked open, its contents covering Mumbum's head – and Bogpipes shot him with a five-pipe stun ray, sending him into the crew of recovering crocs.

"Do as Sam says, laddie!" Moira shouted. "Run!"

Niall turned on his heel and did as

she commanded.

The delta blasts had reminded him of something Sam told him when fixing the Pyra-Base shield: *Take care never to spill water on a Crystal of Ra — or it will explode, KA-BOOM!*

And that had given him a desperate idea . . .

Splashing along the corridor, Niall reached the sloping tunnel with the stone hatchway in the bed of the loch and found the opening switch. Of course, when the hatch was last opened, energy shields held back the water.

This time, there would be nothing to contain the water . . .

170

Bracing himself, Niall hit the switch and the sandstone entrance above scraped open.

All at once, dark, freezing water did its best Niagara Falls impression, flooding inside at incredible speed!

"Whoaaaaaaa!" Niall cried as the tsunami struck like a giant's punch and sent him flying headlong back down the tunnel!

I knew this plan was crazy, he thought, *but this is a whole other league of bonkers!* As he tumbled and splashed and fought for breath, he caught a crazy corkscrew glimpse of Sobek's lair fast approaching . . . He saw Moira and Sam

 171

clinging together as the evil croc-god loomed over them . . . and there was Mumbum and the crowd of crocodiles, directly in his path, jaws wide and waiting.

Niall squeezed his eyes shut.

The freezing water stunned the crocs

the second it hit them. Mumbum was caught out too, his paw-jets put out by the titanic torrent. He and the crocs spun away like scaly poos in the mother of all toilet-flushes.

"WHAT IS THE MEANING OF THIS?" Sobek shouted as the icy water whooshed in. "The crystals will fuse and break if the water hits them . . ." He pointed at the oncoming floods as the glow from the pyramid of crystals grew brighter . . .

Suddenly the rushing water was being swept back *out* of Sobek's throne room – taking Sam, Moira, Bogpipes and the crocodiles with it!

Niall found himself travelling in reverse along the passage, riding the crest of an impossible wave. "Just as I'd hoped, he's used one of his shields to push the water out of his throne room!"

"Most ingenious, my young friend," Sam shouted. "Now, quick! Hold hands!"

"This is no time for soppy stuff!" Moira protested as the water pulled them up the

174

tunnel towards the hatch. "Och, ye'll be trying to snog me, next!"

"I most certainly will not!" Sam cried, as the hatch leading to the loch bed raced nearer. "I am meaning, let us not get separated by the wat-*ERRRRRRRR!*"

Niall just had time to grab Sam's bandaged fingers before Sobek's power expelled the water at high speed back into the loch! They tumbled through the magical current, swimming upward with all their strength.

"We did it!" Sam shouted as he burst through the surface of the loch into the

 175

sunlight. "We have escaped!"

"Aye!" Moira splashed up just beside Niall, Bogpipes at her side as ever, somehow treading water with his pipes. "We're out of Sobek's lair, all right, but so are all those crocky-monsters!"

Niall looked around. Grisly green shapes were bobbing about in the water – and so was croco-Mumbum, floating upside down with his claws in the air.

"We must reach the shore before we are eaten," said Sam, striking out for the grassy banks and the two pyramids beyond.

176

"We'll get there quicker if we travel by Bogpipes." Moira gripped her pet's tartan body. "Tow us in, pet! Top speed!"

Sam and Niall had barely a moment to grab hold before Bogpipes zoomed off like a motorboat, dragging his passengers to the bank, and pulling away from the croc-monsters as they snapped in confusion.

"Splendid work, bag of tartan!" said Sam, getting to his feet. "Now, if we are quick, we can escape in my Pyra-Base."

"And go where? Do what?" Moira followed Sam towards his pyramid, shaking her soggy

bandages. "Sobek's gonna get your Crystal of Ra sooner or later."

"I would Crystal-of-Ra-ther he did not!" Sam slapped Niall on the back. "I joke to keep our spirits up, yes?"

"No," said Niall, who was cold, wet and miserable. "Moira's right. In a world full of crocs, where can we hide?"

"Up a big tree!" Sam suggested. "Or in a hot hair balloon!"

"Hot *air*! Like what you're full of." Moira tutted. "Sobek can turn birds into crocodiles too, remember? They would bite us as

they fell from the sky!"

The Pyra-Base was close now. Sam pulled a pyramid key-fob out of his pocket and hit the door remote. The stone door swung open . . .

But before they could get inside, they bounced off an invisible wall.

"Arrgh!" cried Niall, falling on his wet butt. "Has Mew got the energy shield on?"

"It's not that daft moggy's doing. Look." Moira had turned round, pointing to the loch. "Sobek!"

The waters of the loch were churning and bubbling, parting like aquatic curtains.

179

Contained within the golden bubble of his force field, the enormous crocodile-god rose up from his hidden base in all his gruesome glory.

"You have made me angry, fools!" he thundered. "Now you will die!"

Chapter Twelve

All Change!

"We would very much like not to die, please, Sobek," Sam called to the vengeful god watching from the water. "Perhaps if you just let us into my Pyra-Base—"

"Infantile idiot! You think you would be safe in there?" Sobek uncurled one fist to reveal a piece of papyrus inked with hieroglyphs in his bright blue blood. The golden energy shield

181

faded from his face as he held it to his snout.

With one enormous, gusting snort, Sobek blew it towards the Pyra-Base.

"Uh-oh," said Niall.

The hieroglyphs caught fire and their shadows fluttered from the page like evil birds. They swooped over the top of the energy shield that held Niall, Sam and Moira away from the Pyra-Base, and vanished inside.

182

"Oh dear, crikey!" cried Sam. "Poor Mew! My poor camels!"

"They'll all be turned into crocs, the same as mine." Moira clutched her bandaged head. "Och, there's nothing we can do to stop that brute. It's hopeless."

"Nothing is hopeless, Moira!" Sam told her. "But if we do not ever try, how will we know *what* we can do?"

"You can DIE," cried Sobek, still hovering on the water as his crocodiles crawled out of the loch, sniffing the air. "THAT is what you can do!"

Sam frowned. "I do not think you are getting into the spirit of my highly motivating words, Sobek!"

There was a scuffling, snapping sound from the gloomy hallway of Sam's Pyra-Base. Looking round, Niall felt chilled to his soggy butt to find giant croc-creatures scuttling through the door, tufts of beige fur on their bodies hardening to dark scales.

Sam groaned. "My camels!"

"Look!" Moira pointed to the largest of the croc-monsters. It held Sam's Crystal of Ra in its slavering jaws.

184

"Yes . . . Bring it to me . . ." Sobek threw back his hideous head and laughed like a looper. "At last, the ultimate power will be mine. I will be able to project my Hieroglyphs of Horror all around the globe, changing each and every animal into my crocodile servants!"

"Moira, quick – your Pyra-Base!" Sam led his friends in a charge towards the other pyramid. "Perhaps we can still get away . . ."

But as they neared the doorway, Sam skidded to a halt. Niall, Moira and Bogpipes froze as a small, fat, green, toothy monster stumbled into sight. Golden bandages were wrapped around

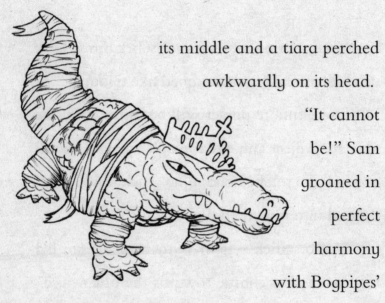

its middle and a tiara perched awkwardly on its head.

"It cannot be!" Sam groaned in perfect harmony with Bogpipes' shocked toot. "Great Mew!"

Niall clutched his head. "The hieroglyphs have turned Mew into Sobek's slave too."

"But what was she doing in *my* Pyra-Base instead of yours?" asked Moira.

186

"I have them, master!" Mew crooned in a spooky voice. "I will bring them to you . . ."

"Excellent!" called Sobek from the loch, the water still parted around him. "You see, mummies? All things are Sobek's to command!"

"I will bring them, master," croco-Mew repeated, scurrying across the grass towards Sobek – right past Sam, Niall and Moira. "I have them, master, I have them . . ."

"What foolishness is this?" Sobek demanded as the funny green shape pushed in front of the croc with the crystal. "You do *not* have them. You have left my prisoners over there!"

187

Suddenly the croco-Mew spat out several pieces of papyrus. "When I said 'I have them,' I wasn't talking about *them*. I was talking about THESE!"

The scraps were marked with distinctive, scrawled symbols . . .

"Impossible! Hieroglyphs of Horror?" Sobek stared in alarm as the symbols seared smokily through the papyrus and their shadows poured out into the air. "What spell is this . . . ?"

"One that *spells* the end of your plans!" cried Mew, watching the hieroglyphs vanish down the maws of the surrounding crocs. "I've cracked

the code of your silly hieroglyphs – and *these* ones ought to unscramble all the scrambling you've done!"

Sobek gave a hiss of rage – and the croc with the crystal gave a hiccup as it accidentally swallowed the stone along with a steaming hieroglyph. "Nooooooo!"

Niall boggled as the crocodiles snapping on the shoreline began to twitch and shake. They sprouted fur. Their snouts shrank. Their butts started sucking in their tails like scaly spaghetti. "Sam, Moira, look – they're changing . . ."

"They are becoming normal once again!"

Sam clapped as the crocodile-creatures shimmered, transforming back into the cats and camels and cows – and even the giraffe – they were before . . . Even Mumbum's bandaged bottom was growing doggier again. "It is a fine miracle!"

"But which one swallowed the crystal?" asked Niall as the camels milled about in confusion.

"I have no idea, my friend," said Sam. "Let us hope Sobek does not know either!"

Moira's mouth was agape. "How is this even happening?"

The question was clearly perplexing Sobek too. "How can this be, cat-goddess?" he bellowed down at the croco-Mew. "Your worthless body was changed by my hieroglyphs . . . And now I shall crush you underfoot!" As if to prove his point, he stamped down on the fat green

191

body. Niall and Sam gasped . . .

But as her scaly body squashed flat, a scrawny white figure squirted out and fled towards Sam like a scalded cat . . .

"Mew!" Niall was beyond gobsmacked. "It's the real you!"

"Of course it's the real me-*owww!* Who were you expecting – Nefertiti?" Mew cowered behind Sam's legs, although for now it seemed she was safe – Sobek was busy with the newly freed animals, transfixing each one with his huge eyes, staring into their very souls. "Which of you has the Crystal of Ra? WHICH?"

Happy hunting, ugly, thought Niall. But he knew that a creature with Sobek's powers wouldn't stay bamboozled for long.

"A fine deception, Great Mew." Sam smiled with sudden understanding. "You were never changed into a real crocodile, were you?"

"No," Moira agreed. "She just wriggled inside my *stuffed* crocodile from the Pyra-Base!"

"Having found the revolting thing, I thought I should put it to good use," Mew agreed. "I mourn the loss of my golden wrappings and tiara, but I had to get close to Sobek's crocs to

193

stand the best chance of changing them back."

Niall went on staring at the various animals dashing through the heather as Sobek screamed after them in wild fury. "How *did* you turn them all back?"

"Once the Rosetta Ray cracked the code and translated the symbols, I was able to create my own unscrambling spell in hieroglyphs!"

Sam winced. "In your own blood, Great Mew?"

"Yes. I'm the only goddess I know!" She held up a limp paw to reveal a blue pinprick. "The sacrifices I make, just to save the fish— um,

planet!" she corrected herself quickly. "Save the planet, I mean, yes. Now, quickly, before Sobek can make new hieroglyphs to counter mine – you mummies must distract him." A crafty glint appeared in her green eyes. "Sobek controls the energy shields with brain-power. He needs to concentrate. Now, if that concentration were broken . . ."

"He would have no shield," Niall realized, "and we could really hit him hard!"

"HA!" Sobek boomed. The crocodile-god was still hovering above the loch, and one of the camels was stuck inside another force-shield

195

bubble. "YOU
swallowed the
crystal!"

Moira grimaced.
"Now we're for it."

Sobek looked
over at Mew. "Your

interference is meaningless, cat-goddess!" He pricked the end of one finger on a tooth, then started to furiously scrawl hieroglyphs on a piece of papyrus. "I shall soon undo your work with new, stronger hieroglyphs! My might WILL overcome all."

"Quickly, everyone," Mew hissed. "Here's what I want you to do . . ."

She outlined her plan. Niall gulped. Bog-pipes tooted. Sam tooted too (which was quite understandable in the circumstances).

"All right," said Moira nervously. "I guess I'm up for distracting him if you are, Sam."

"Yes!" Sam raised a bandaged fist. "If this is to be our final battle . . . BRING IT OFF!"

"*On*," Niall corrected him. But the mummies, along with Bogpipes, were already charging away across the heather, scattering the menagerie of leftover animals. Sobek didn't seem to notice, he

was absorbed in his hieroglyphic work, his energy shield still parting the water all the way back to the stone hatch that led down to his base.

"Hey, Sobek!" Sam shouted, a pyramid-grenade in both hands. "Catch!" He hurled the small, white missiles.

BOOM! Ka-BLAM! They exploded against Sobek's personal shield. He didn't even look up from his hieroglyphs.

"Get him, Bogpipes!" Moira cried. While her tartan pet fired his rays at Sobek, she shook her legs until a pair of

dark wooden swords popped up from the bandages around her hips. "Hey! They're the first ebony blades I've made in two thousand years!"

"Very nice craftsmanship! Kindly use them!" Sam called as he raised sandstorms and dust devils from his fingers and blasted them at Sobek's scaly head. Moira gave a shrill battle cry and started chopping at the croco-god's legs.

Sandstorms, swords, stun-rays, grenades — Niall watched as the weapons raged around Sobek in a supercharged onslaught. Still the evil crocodile-god remained untouched in his

199

golden bubble. How long before his spell was finished? Niall wondered . . .

"Now, Niall!" Mew urged him. "You must play your part quickly – before it's too late!"

Chapter Thirteen

To Battle a God –
and Eat a Cod

Heart pounding like a drumbeat at a disco, Niall ran towards the waters of the loch, where Mumbum floated near the shore. "Are you all right, boy?"

Mumbum's bandaged tail wagged weakly.

"Let's hope we're both still all right by the time we've sneaked past scaly-face!" He lifted

the metal mutt-butt and carried him towards the battleground. "We're on a mission!"

Still busy with distraction tactics, Sam was hurling more pyramid-grenades at Sobek, while Moira fired delta force blasts. Bogpipes was jumping up and down on the crocodile god's head. But Sobek remained absorbed in his hieroglyphs; he did not notice Niall, with Mumbum in his arms, hurrying past him towards the stone hatchway. The walls of water shimmered on either side of

him as he skidded and squelched through the thick sandy muck of the loch bed. Finally he reached the entrance to the submerged Pyra-Base.

"I need you to blast open this hatch, boy," Niall whispered. "Quickly but quietly."

The chunky bionic battle-suit hummed with power as the bum behind it got ready to rock. *ZAM-ZAM-ZAM!* The gun nozzle fired blast after blast of bright blue fire at the stone slab. The hatch crumbled and broke up like a wet sugar cube, revealing blackness within.

Stage one of the plan was complete!

The pieces of hatch crackled against an invisible force field blocking the way beneath. Mew had predicted as much – that was why distracting Sobek was vital. "No one can get at his crystals while he's up here," Niall murmured. "Not unless he loses concentration . . ."

Could Sam and Moira make that happen? Together with Bogpipes, they were still hurling all they had at Sobek – but he remained safe inside his bubble of energy. Niall and Mumbum scurried back past him in the opposite direction, slipping as they

scrambled up the slope to the grassy shore.

"Och, it's no use, Sam!" Moira fired a flurry of quill darts at Sobek, but they bounced off uselessly. "We can't touch him."

"It is time for a change in tactics!" Sam declared. "Hey, Sobek! Is it true that your mother was so ugly she made the sphinxes be sick whenever they saw her?"

Sobek hissed angrily – then went on writing. "You cannot distract me. These hieroglyphs are so strong, no one will ever be able to undo their dark magic."

Sam tried again. "Is it true that the feet of

205

your mother smelled so bad they made camels explode?"

Sobek's right eye flickered. "I . . . I do not heed the insults of insects."

But Sam wasn't stopping now: "I heard that the bottom of your mother was so very big, she knocked over pyramids each time she did the bending over—"

"THAT'S IT!" Sobek rounded on Sam, eyes burning like miniature suns. A hole opened in his shield as he blasted Sam with optic energy, sending the mummy to the ground in a smoking heap . . .

"Sam!" Niall cried.

Taking full advantage of the hole in the energy shield, Moira threw one last quill at Sobek – the biggest quill of all. Its razor-sharp point shot right up the monster's nostril.

"OWWWWWWWWWW!" he screamed.

A split-second later, Bogpipes dived in and jammed a pipe up the other nostril, then opened fire with an atomic *TOOT!*

"GAHHHHHH!" Clutching his crocodile conk in pain, Sobek's concentration was finally broken.

His energy shields melted away!

He fell into the loch with a splash.

The camel with the crystal was released from its glowing prison and galloped off, straight for Moira's Pyra-Base.

At the same time, the waters of the loch

surged back together. Only now, thanks to Niall's work with Mumbum, the entrance to the secret base had been blown open. Tons of loch-water flooded down into the chamber below . . .

Without Sobek's energy to turn back the tides, Niall knew that the water level in his underground lair would be rising higher and higher. But right now he had other things on his mind. "Sam!" He rushed over to his fallen friend. "Are you all right?"

"My bandages are bruised and battered — but still I live!" Sam's eyes snapped open.

209

"What a touchy god that Sobek is!"

"Aye, ye found a weak spot there, Sam." Moira pulled him to his feet and slapped him on the back. "And Bogpipes and I found one more – right up the schnozzle!"

"You interfering microbes!" Sobek had recovered, and was once more encased in his protective bubble. He had pulled the quill from his swollen nostril, and his eyes were narrowed with hatred. "No one has attacked me for three thousand years – and no one ever will again! I am ready to unleash the final hieroglyphs on the world!"

"Uh-oh," said Niall, with a nervous look at Sam. Great Mew bounded over to join them, and Mumbum and Bogpipes huddled together in fear.

"There!" Sobek put the papyrus to his jaws. "The spell is primed! Now, with a single breath, it shall be released!"

Niall, Sam and Moira waited tensely for the glow to disappear, for Sobek's deadly breath to blow the hieroglyphs into the air . . .

But the glow only grew brighter.

"I . . . I cannot turn off my shield!" Sobek shouted. "What stupidity is this?"

211

"I think you will find it is your stupidity."
Mew smiled. "While you were hopping about
with feathers up your hooter, water flooded
into your base . . . causing the Crystals of Ra to
short-circuit!"

"Then . . . this shield is fused?" Sobek
gasped, and hammered against the glowing
bubble all around him. "No! I have made the
hieroglyphs devastatingly strong, enough to
transform an entire *world* of animals. If they
are released into this tiny space around me,
with no room to spread . . ."

But the papyrus was already smoking.

Sobek's energy shield was filling fast with a seething swarm of symbols, thousands and thousands of them. Millions and millions!

And they had nowhere to go but into Sobek's body – changing it, charging it, messing it up.

"NOOOOOOOOOOO!" Sobek groaned as his great crocodile head rippled and billowed.

213

His muscles melted. His scaly skin crumpled. And still the Hieroglyphs of Horror multiplied, their darkness dissolving Sobek into nothing but a final terrifying scream . . .

The smoking symbols died away, leaving no trace of anything at all.

The waters of the loch began to bubble and boil.

"Everybody take cover!" Mew shouted. "Sobek's waterlogged Crystals of Ra are overloading. There's going to be the most wonderful explosion!"

"Wonderful?" Sam frowned. "What do

you mean, Great Mew?"

Mew pulled her tiara and bandages off Moira's stuffed crocodile and scarpered. "You'll see!"

"Bogpipes, get herding these animals into our Pyra-Base," Moira commanded, and her pet got to work. "Mumbum, help too."

"*WOOF!*" Mumbum agreed, his paw-jets sputtering back to life, tail wagging happily from side to side as he and Bogpipes saw the animals safely to shelter.

Niall sprinted after them. He had almost made it to the pyramid when a whopping blast

knocked him off his feet and hurled him into the heather. He watched as a gigantic surge of water was blasted upward from the grey loch . . . then groaned as it fell down like heavy rain, thick with fish!

"*That's* what I meant by wonderful!" Mew hungrily chomped down a large salmon. "Mmmmm, fresh fish cooked in a supernatural explosion. There's nothing finer! MIAOWW-WWWW!"

Niall smiled at her. "Mew, you were, like, totally a hero today!"

"True." She nodded. "Cometh the hour,

cometh the cat-goddess. I mean, just imagine if all the fish in the world became ghastly crocodiles! Dear me, that would never do!"

"Well, whatever your reasons, cat, ye put things right." Moira bowed to her. "I s'pose I was wrong about you."

"And what about you, Moira?" Sam asked. "You fought most well! Will you come out of retirement and join me in seeking out other criminals from KaBa that hide on the Earth?"

"Are you crazy?" Moira stared at him. "You want me to help you out, when I could be tucked up in a lovely bed of heather

and thistles, eating porridge? No way!" She paused, then smiled too. "Although, if ye really need me . . . ye know where ye can find me."

"My thanks, noble McMummy." Sam bowed to her, then turned to Niall. "And you, my friend? I hope I can still count on your help?"

"Course you can, Sam," said Niall. "Except for in just one thing."

"Oh?" Sam blinked. "And what is this thing?"

Niall grinned. "I am NOT helping you sort

through camel poo until you find the last ever Crystal of Ra! Mum will be wondering where I am . . . and after coming up against Sobek and his scaly mates, being stuck with the Snitch doesn't seem quite so bad after all!"

will return in

THE GHOST OF TUTANKHAMUN

MYSTERIES OF ANCIENT EGYPT

With your wise guide and hostess – Great Mew

(most beloved of Bastet the cat goddess)

MIAOWWW! Some of the Ancient Egyptian things in this book may seem strange to you. You are, after all, just a stupid human! So let me grab a quick fish and explain ...

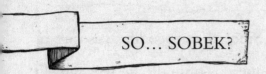

SO... SOBEK?

First of all, can you guess what the name 'Sobek' means? Crocodile – fancy that! Mentions of Sobek go back as far as Old Kingdom Egypt. That's 4,500 years ago!

Even older than my pants!

The Ancient Egyptians believed that Sobek was both good and bad – and very powerful. It was believed the entire River Nile was formed

from his sweat! Since the crocodile was one of Egypt's most dangerous animals, he was widely worshipped. In many temples you could find pools with crocodiles who were fed meat, honey and cake and then mummified when they died. Yes, people would do whatever they could to keep Sobek on their side!

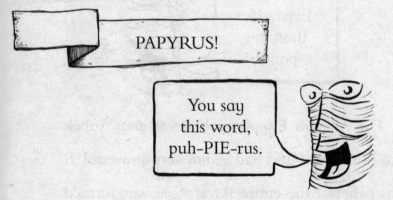

PAPYRUS!

You say this word, puh-PIE-rus.

The Hieroglyphs of Horror were written on papyrus. In real Ancient Egyptian life, papyrus was very important. People believed that the papyrus plant grew on the mound of creation. It certainly grew very quickly in the marshy Nile mud! It was used for rope, parts of it could be eaten and its flowers were given as an offering to the gods!

Bet you never got any, cat!

Silence, boy! I was after fish, not flowers . . .

225

The oldest papyrus used for writing dates all the way back to 3035 BC and was found in a tomb. Making a piece of papyrus was a long process. Strips of the plant stalks were beaten and bound together to make sheets, then when the sheets were dry, they were ready to be made into rolls.

Those who could afford papyrus wrote on the inside. Papyrus with writing on the outside had probably been reused by the poor – an early example of paper recycling, MIAOOOWWW!

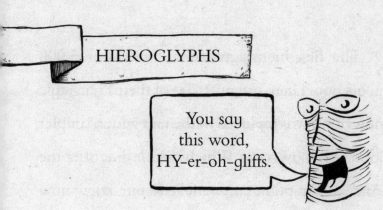

HIEROGLYPHS

You say this word, HY-er-oh-gliffs.

A hieroglyph is a written character that looks like a picture. 'Hieroglyph' is actually a Greek word, meaning 'sacred carving'. The Egyptians called hieroglyphs *mdju netjer*, meaning 'words of the gods'.

What a mouthful!

The first hieroglyphs date from over 5,000 years ago. There are over 700 of them! This style of writing was replaced in the end with a simpler kind of handwriting. Which meant that after the Ancient Egyptian empire fell, no one knew how to translate all those 'sacred signs'.

It wasn't until the Rosetta Stone was discovered in 1799 that things changed. Back in 196 BC, this special stone had been carved with the same royal decree in three different languages

– including hieroglyphs! By comparing the hieroglyphs to the languages they could read, experts learned to understand the mysterious symbols once more.

They should have asked a clever cat who was there at the time – MEEEEE!

Great Mew would like to thank the human Ancient Egypt Advisor Louise Ellis-Barrett for her help with this section.

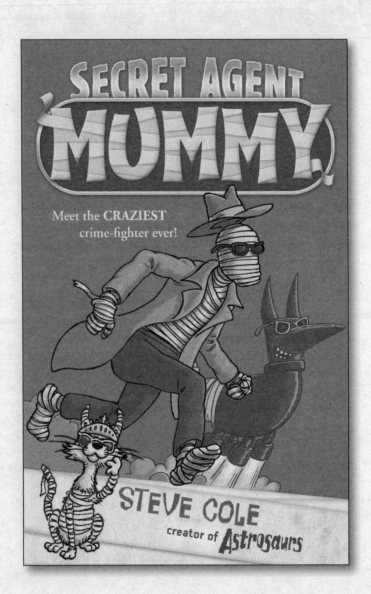

SECRET AGENT MUMMY

Meet the **CRAZIEST**
crime-fighter ever!

STEVE COLE

creator of **Astrosaurs**

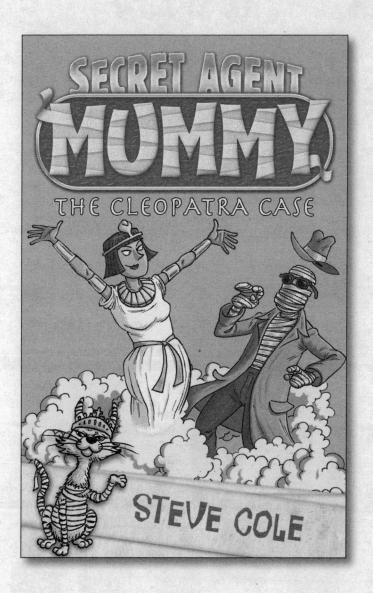

DINOSAURS... IN SPACE!

Meet Captain Teggs Stegosaur and the crew of the amazing spaceship DSS *Sauropod* as the ASTROSAURS fight evil across the galaxy!